DM

THE GOLDEN LURE

Working as companion to a crotchety elderly lady, Ella Matthews' existence is brightened by her brother's letters telling her of his adventures on the goldfields of Australia. When he invites her to join him she's thrilled to go and experience some adventures herself. But arriving in Melbourne, she's stranded, alone and fearing for her brother's safety. The only man she can turn to is journalist Nathaniel Lake. Will he agree to let her accompany him to the goldfields?

KATHERINE LANGTON

THE GOLDEN LURE

Complete and Unabridged

LINFORD
Leicester

First published in Great Britain in 2010

First Linford Edition
published 2011

British Library CIP Data

Langton, Katherine.
  The golden lure. - -
  (Linford romance library)
  1. Brothers and sisters- -Fiction. 2. Young
  women- -Australia- -Melbourne (Vic.)- -
  Fiction. 3. Gold miners- -Australia- -
  Fiction. 4. Journalists- -Fiction. 5. Love
  stories. 6. Large type books.
  I. Title II. Series
  823.9′2–dc22

  ISBN 978–1–4448–0891–9

Published by
F. A. Thorpe (Publishing)
Anstey, Leicestershire

Set by Words & Graphics Ltd.
Anstey, Leicestershire
Printed and bound in Great Britain by
T. J. International Ltd., Padstow, Cornwall

1

'So I really must ask you for this week's rent, Miss Matthews. Now, it's not in my nature to press a lady, but this here establishment ain't no charity. I'm sure you understand. What with everybody haring off to the goldfields the way they are, we, the hardworking, decent people left behind, need to earn a crust . . . Oh — thank you, miss. Much obliged.'

Ella Matthews closed the door behind Mr Tingley, the landlord, and leaned her forehead on it. Her room was safe for another week, but her funds were now dangerously low. She wondered what she would eat tonight — or, perhaps, the question should properly be should she eat at all, for Ella did not know how she was going to pay for a meal.

Not for the first time, she wondered if she would not have been wiser to have stayed in England and kept her post as companion to the crotchety and demanding Mrs Pugh. She had not been particularly fond of her employer — nor had Mrs Pugh been fond of her — but Ella's position had meant she was assured of a roof over her head and three meals a day.

In hindsight, her days with Mrs Pugh were a secure paradise compared to the uncertainty she was now facing. Ella was on the other side of the world, in Melbourne, Australia, in the midst of what was becoming known as the Gold Rush.

Disembarking from the ship, she had not known what to expect. Melbourne was a town only eighteen years old. The streets were still largely unformed, unlit and unpaved. There were buildings — some even built of stone — but the economy had come to a standstill.

It was as if Melbourne Town had died. No more building was taking place, and the few shops still trading, no matter if they were milliners, confectioners, or linen drapers, all seemed to trade in gold, while their legitimate business had become nothing more than a sideline.

Ella thought that every person in Melbourne had become unhinged with gold fever. With her own position so precarious, alone and almost penniless, it was not a comforting notion.

Victoria was a new colony, only separated from New South Wales two years before in 1850. Ella had recently read in a newspaper a mock dispatch from Governor LaTrobe, complaining that because all his staff had decamped to the goldfields, he was now obliged to clean his own boots, groom his own horse, and chop his own wood. But the situation was becoming desperate, as it was common knowledge that Governor LaTrobe feared for the future of the fledging colony.

However, at the present moment Ella was more concerned with her own situation. If her brother Christopher did not send for her soon, she would somehow have to find employment in this town on the brink of economic collapse. Melbourne was already swamped with hundreds of destitute people; Ella knew she could easily join their number.

She could end up in Canvas Town. Ella shuddered at the thought. She had glimpsed Canvas Town on her journey into Melbourne after leaving the docks. As its name implied, it was a town of tents; rows and rows inhabited by broken and destitute people. Many were women; some widowed, some deserted by their men. There were also children living there. Ella had discovered that many husbands and fathers had abandoned their families to their fate when they went to seek their fortune on the goldfields, while unsuccessful gold-seekers, their energy, hope and initiative sapped, their health destroyed, also eventually found themselves in Canvas Town.

And there many of them seemed to stay, drinking away their last pennies.

Ella shuddered again. Was that to be

her lot? Squalor and despair? She vowed it would not, but the day she was unable to pay her bill would be the day Mr Tingley threw her out of the hotel — and it wouldn't be long in coming.

For the first time in her life, Ella was frightened, truly frightened. Even when her parents had died, leaving her and her brother Christopher almost penniless, she couldn't recall having been this frightened. And she had brought this situation upon herself! Ella knew no one in Melbourne.

Where are you, Christopher? she fretted silently. Why hadn't he sent her a message? Why hadn't he called for her, as he had promised?

Christopher had written so persuasively, asking Ella to resign her post and undertake the long and arduous journey to Australia to join him in his search for gold. But since arriving here six weeks ago, apart from the short letter he had left for her with Mr Tingley telling her to stay at the hotel until he should come to collect her, Ella had had no word from him. All she knew was that her brother had been heading for Ballarat, where gold had been discovered the year before, in 1851.

Sitting down on her bed, Ella counted out her remaining coins. She was down to her last few shillings. She stared around her almost bare room. It was very small, and contained only a metal-framed bed, a chair and a small rickety table. She suspected Mr Tingley was overcharging her, but she was reluctant to challenge him, for fear of being tossed out into the street.

Dragging the chair to the window, Ella stared out at the quiet street. A solitary wagon passed by, the horse dragging it at a plodding pace. Her six-week stay at the hotel had eaten away her funds. She could no longer rely on Christopher to rescue her.

Ella forced herself to consider the possibility that something might have happened to her brother. He could be ill, or even . . . Her mind skittered away from that thought, but she wondered if Christopher, having failed in his search for gold, was himself in Canvas Town, or some other place like it. The letter he had left for her was dated nearly three months earlier. He could be anywhere. Discoveries of gold were taking place all over Victoria, each new discovery eclipsing the last.

Ella's stomach grumbled; she felt slightly dizzy and was glad that she was seated. She had been rationing herself severely, trying to make her money last as long as possible. All she had had today was a thin slice of unbuttered bread and a cup of weak tea. Ella knew she would become ill if she didn't eat properly, and then how could she look for work?

She didn't know with whom she felt angrier, herself or her brother. In all the letters Christopher had written to her, he had never even hinted that there were such places as Canvas Town. All he had told her was that there were fortunes to be made in Victoria, and he was determined to make his!

Should she look for Christopher? Victoria was a big place. Besides, she had no funds to embark on a search. No, she would do better to stay in Melbourne and try and find employment. When she had money in her purse, then she would consider a search for Christopher.

Having come to this decision, Ella nodded to herself. Sitting here staring out of the window and fretting wouldn't get her a job. She would have to go out and start asking people if they had work available.

Her stomach rumbled again as she got to her feet. While she was out, she would beg some stale bread or a piece of pie from the baker's down the street . . . and perhaps, if she were lucky, the baker would offer her a job. She would sweep the floors if she had to.

Putting on her bonnet and throwing a shawl around her shoulders, Ella left her room. It surprised her what a

Herculean effort it took to walk down the stairs. Reaching the lobby, another wash of dizziness overcame her. Ella swayed. She felt herself falling, and the next moment everything went black.

* * *

'She's coming around. Hand me the tea!'

Ella felt the rim of a teacup pressed to her lips. Her eyes still closed, and barely conscious of her surroundings, she sipped the warm liquid. All she was aware of was how tired and hungry and thirsty she was.

The tea, unlike the weak, watery brew she had drunk that morning, was strong, milky and very sweet. She took a bigger sip, grateful for the warmth that slid down her throat. When she had drunk it all, she looked up to discover a dark-haired man gazing down at her, his grey eyes regarding her with concern. She was lying on the floor, her head cradled on his left arm. Her bonnet was lying on the floor by her side.

Ella blinked up at him in confusion. She had been going out to look for work . . . How had she come to be lying on the floor?

'I won't have no sickness in this here establishment!' Mr Tingley's petulant tones cut into Ella's confusion. 'If Miss Matthews is ill, she'll have to go elsewhere. This ain't a hospital!'

'The girl's not sick, but half-starved. Use your eyes, Tingley!' The man looked back down at Ella. 'I've asked the housekeeper to boil some eggs for you. They should be here shortly. If I help you, do you think you can stand?'

'I . . . I think so.' She was a little wobbly on her feet, but with the man's assistance, she was able to walk to the room that served as a dining parlour.

'What happened?' she asked weakly.

'You fainted.' The man pulled out a chair for her, and gratefully Ella sat down. The tea had restored her somewhat. She studied her rescuer.

He was tall and dark-haired, his skin lightly tanned — and he was a complete stranger. She hadn't seen him around the hotel before — she would have remembered him if she had! He must have arrived late yesterday, or perhaps even early this morning. She recalled hearing the sounds of an arrival in the early hours.

Who was he? Before she could ask, the housekeeper bustled in carrying a tray. Not only had she brought the two boiled eggs as promised, but there were also several slices of buttered toast and a jug of chocolate.

The smell of the food made Ella's mouth water. 'Oh!'

'When was the last time you ate, Miss Matthews?' The man sat himself across from her, although the housekeeper placed no food in front of him. Carrying her tray, the housekeeper left the room, but Mr Tingley remained at the doorway. Despite her hunger, Ella noted his aggrieved expression.

He's probably wondering if I'm going

to pay for this meal, she thought. She dropped her hands to her lap to stop herself from snatching at the toast, because the truth was that she couldn't.

Her rescuer looked at her sternly. 'Eat,' he ordered.

Ella shook her head. 'I cannot . . . that is . . . '

The man made an exasperated sound. He turned to the hovering Mr Tingley. 'Are you accustomed to frightening all your guests in this manner?'

'I've a living to earn, Mr Lake,' Mr Tingley retorted. 'This hotel ain't a charity, and what with the way things are . . . I'm sure you understand — just as Miss Matthews here does. She pays her rent so I let her stay, but I'm not her guardian.'

Mr Lake gave Mr Tingley a level look. 'I see.' There was a wealth of meaning in those two little words. 'Well, you may rely on me to settle Miss Matthews' bill.'

Mr Tingley still looked suspicious.

'Be sure you do, Mr Lake. I have a living to earn,' he repeated with emphasis, and stomped from the room.

'Mr Lake, it's very kind of you, but I cannot possibly — ' Ella began.

'You can and you will, Miss Matthews. Now eat, please, before the food gets cold.'

Ella hesitated, but the sight of the food laid out before her was too much. She picked up a knife and sliced off the top of an egg. She felt very self-conscious eating in front of a stranger — a stranger, moreover, who had promised to pay for her meal. However was she to pay him back? She would have to think of something.

When she had finished the egg and eaten a piece of toast, she spoke again. 'You must think me very foolish.'

'Not at all. I am not aware of your circumstances, so I can hardly judge.'

Ella picked up a second slice of toast and nibbled it. 'I did eat this morning, but . . . '

'Evidently not enough — and if I'm

any judge, you haven't been eating properly for some weeks.' He looked at her severely. 'Pale and interesting may be all the rage in London, but this is not the time or place to take ill. There are no doctors in Melbourne, or none that I would recommend! Like everyone else, they've contracted this disease called gold fever — for which there's no cure, it seems.'

'I assure you, the last thing I wish to do is make myself ill,' Ella rejoined. 'Particularly as I am seeking employment.'

'Hmm.' Mr Lake was silent while Ella finished her toast and drank another cup of tea. 'Are you feeling better now?' he enquired.

Ella nodded. 'Immensely.' Never had she eaten a better meal! 'Thank you, Mr Lake. As soon as I secure employment, I will repay you.'

Mr Lake looked sceptical; although whether it was at her statement of finding employment or paying him back, Ella was unsure.

'What brings you — clearly a gently brought-up young lady — here?' he asked. 'Tingley tells me you arrived alone. Melbourne isn't the place for lone gentlewomen at this time. I strongly recommend you return to your family.'

'My family is here.'

Mr Lake looked disbelieving. 'You look fresh off the boat to me.'

'I arrived six weeks ago to be with my family, which consists of my only brother. He is, or was, in Ballarat. I was intending to search for him, but — '

Mr Lake did not let her finish. 'Miss Matthews, you cannot possibly travel to Ballarat!' He looked appalled. 'And I doubt you'd find your brother if you did. There are thousands of men on the goldfields. You have no idea what conditions are like. The diggings are no place for a young gentlewoman.'

Although grateful for his care of her, this second reference to her being a gentlewoman needled Ella. Mr Lake made her sound as if she were a pampered duke's daughter doing the Grand Tour!

'It's a good thing, then, Mr Lake, that I am not a gentlewoman, by nature or by nurture. Nor am I particularly young. I am four-and-twenty, which puts me firmly on the shelf; besides which, I have been earning my own living for five years — working for a very demanding elderly lady!'

Mr Lake's eyebrows had shot upwards during her tirade. 'My apologies, Miss Matthews. I see I have offended you, but I assumed you were — well, to put it bluntly, adventuring. I've met many such this past year, although the adventurers I've met tend to be young men, mostly idle younger sons of wealthy families out for a lark, and various other ne'er-do-wells.'

Ella did not reply. Although his comments had annoyed her, she sensed that Mr Lake knew what he was talking about — and he was nearly right. Her brother Christopher could almost be described as an adventurer — only the wealthy family part was missing!

She studied Mr Lake, suddenly coming to the realisation that he wasn't English. He did not speak quite the way she did, nor did he look 'fresh off the boat', being tanned and somewhat rough around the edges. He also appeared to know this country well.

How well? Was she speaking to a convict — or should that be ex-convict? She couldn't imagine the uptight Mr Tingley harbouring a runaway criminal.

Realising the turn her thoughts had taken, Ella hastily looked down. Alas, Mr Lake read her thoughts with unerring accuracy.

'If it will satisfy your curiosity, Miss Matthews, I can assure you I left my ball and chain in Sydney.'

Ella felt her face redden. 'I am sorry. I should not have made such an assumption . . . ' She stumbled to a stop, acutely conscious that she was making things worse. Mr Lake was the first person, and perhaps the only person, who could help her!

Yet weren't convicts evil people? Ella had always believed so. They were sent to Australia for committing crimes, sometimes heinous crimes.

Or was Mr Lake offended that she had assumed he was a convict simply because he was Australian? Many free settlers had emigrated to forge a new life for themselves. Not every Australian had a convict past.

Ella wished the floor would open and swallow her up.

After an uncomfortable silence, Mr Lake spoke again. 'How do you know your brother is — what is his name, by the way?' He clearly had no intention of enlightening her as to his status.

'Christopher,' Ella told him. 'Mine is Ella.'

Mr Lake made no response to that. 'How do you know for certain that your brother Christopher is in Ballarat, Miss Matthews?'

'I have to confess I don't. When I arrived, Mr Tingley handed me a letter Christopher had left for me. In it, he said he was travelling to Ballarat, as he hadn't found much gold where he had been working and Ballarat seemed more promising. He also told me he would write again, but he hasn't.'

'Your brother has been here for some while?'

Ella nodded. 'Yes. He's been in Australia for nearly a year.'

'And you only six weeks. He should have a greater care for you! I suppose it was his idea that you travel out here?'

Ella chewed her lip. 'Yes,' she admitted reluctantly. 'He knew I wasn't happy working for Mrs Pugh and . . . '

'And you wanted to see the world and have adventures. Am I right?'

'Well, why should I not, Mr Lake?' Ella looked at Mr Lake challengingly. 'And if my brother and I find ourselves a fortune, so much the better!'

'This country certainly offers opportunities for those willing to take risks and work hard, Miss Matthews. However, I don't believe anyone — apart from a lucky few — will find what they're seeking for on the goldfields.'

'Perhaps you are right, Mr Lake,' Ella was forced to concede.

'And so, Miss Matthews, you find yourself adrift in a strange country.' Mr Lake steepled his fingers and regarded her solemnly. 'You have rashly left the employment of your Mrs Pugh, and you are stranded and alone — and if I guess correctly, your funds are low. What are your intentions?'

Ella took a breath. 'What I would really like to do is discover what has become of Christopher, but I realise that is impractical. So for now I will seek employment.'

Mr Lake nodded. 'You must know your chances of finding employment in Melbourne are slim. However, I may have a solution that will suit both of us. You, Miss Matthews, can work for me.'

2

Ella stared with incredulity at Mr Lake. 'Work for *you*, sir? What, pray, would you have me do?'

'Indeed. I'm a journalist from Sydney, and my paper sends me to Victoria at regular intervals to report on this phenomenon called the Gold Rush. Unfortunately, on my last tour of duty, the editor complained — vociferously, I might add! — about my abominable handwriting. I generally send my articles off so quickly that they are practically scrawled. If you are able to decipher my scribbled notes and write them out in a neat hand, the job is yours. We can negotiate your fee. What do you say, Miss Matthews? Do you accept?'

Ella gaped. This was certainly a day of surprises! But this offer was a godsend, and she gave the only answer possible.

'Yes, Mr Lake. I accept.'

Such a thing would never have happened in England! Secretaries and office assistants were male, but here in Australia, like the weather, everything was topsy-turvy. Besides, what other choice did she have?

Ella briefly wondered what Mrs Pugh, a stickler for convention, would have thought of her former companion becoming Mr Lake's amanuensis. She would certainly have disapproved! But Mrs Pugh and her disapproval were hundreds of miles away. Ella was free to take whatever position suited her, and this position, she suspected, would be a very interesting one.

Tentatively she asked, 'Have you been to Ballarat before?'

'Twice,' Mr Lake told her. 'I've been to a number of other goldfields as well. I not only write about the successful diggers — that's the Australian name for miners — and the latest gold discoveries, but also the effect on the local economy and those diggers who have failed. Only the lucky few come away from the goldfields drenched with riches. Unfortunately, it's far more common to see deserted families left penniless, and ex-diggers begging on the street. Failures outweigh the success stories.'

'Yes, I've seen instances of both extremes myself.' Ella shuddered, again remembering Canvas Town. Thanks to Mr Lake, that wouldn't be her destination today! 'Why, the day after I arrived here, right outside this hotel I actually saw a man light up a cigar using a twenty-pound note! I still cannot believe it!' She shook her head in wonder at the memory.

Mr Lake smiled wryly. 'Yes, I have seen things like that too. It's usually either ostentatious wealth or the complete opposite.

'Now, if you have finished eating, I suggest you spend the remainder of the day resting. You can join me for dinner tonight, and tomorrow afternoon I should have some work for you to do.'

★ ★ ★

One of Ella's duties in Mrs Pugh's employment had been to read the newspapers aloud to her, so Ella had a little knowledge, like much of Britain, of the Australian gold discoveries. The Times had even hailed the discovery as 'one of the most important events of our time.'

Christopher had been so enchanted by the reports of gold discoveries that he had abruptly left his clerking position to try his luck. His early letters to his sister had been positive. Reading them over, Ella now realised how guarded the later ones had become. Christopher must have had his eyes opened to reality, yet he was sparing in what he revealed to her.

Her rescuer's reports added to Ella's education about the Gold Rush. As he had told her, Mr Lake — Nathaniel, as she discovered his name was — did write about successful gold seekers, and it was heart-warming to read of people who, having travelled across the world seeking a better life, had found it. But he wrote even more eloquently about the unfortunates: the widows, wives and children deserted, diggers injured in mining accidents, and the sheer bad luck stories.

Nor did all successes have a happy outcome. Many diggers, unused to great wealth, became easy prey for conmen and the lures of drink and gambling.

The days passed, and there was still no letter from Christopher. Although Ella was kept busy transcribing Nathaniel's articles, thoughts of her brother never left her mind. Somehow, she would have to find a way to travel to Ballarat and search for Christopher.

Ella seldom saw Nathaniel during the day, but they would meet at dinner when he would hand her the notes he had written. After dinner, she would take them up to her room and spend the evening perusing them. Nathaniel's handwriting truly was as appalling as he had said — no wonder his paper was complaining! — but Ella soon became accustomed to it, eventually being able to decipher even the very worst scrawl. After breakfast the following morning, Ella would begin the task of writing them out neatly. She would give her work to Nathaniel that evening, and he would send them on by messenger where they would go by the next boat to Sydney.

Nathaniel helped Ella in other ways as well. On discovering what she had been paying for her room, he declared she had been cheated and forced the landlord to refund her the difference. Mr Tingley stomped and groaned, reiterating that he had a living to earn, but did not dare dispute the matter further. Nathaniel Lake was a good, regular customer who always paid his bill and Mr Tingley did not dare offend him, so he returned Ella's money.

Ella was grateful. With the fee Nathaniel was paying her, she was even managing to build up a small fund.

During their conversations over dinner, Ella told Nathaniel about herself: the unexpected death of her parents, she and Christopher being forced to earn their own living, and her time with Mrs Pugh. Nathaniel remained reticent about his own life, confining his conversation to his journalistic activities. He did not touch on his personal circumstances, and Ella was loath to press him and appear rude and inquisitive.

Ella now doubted that Nathaniel himself was a former convict, but she was beginning to wonder if his parents had been. It was possible. She also remained ignorant as to whether he was married, whether his parents were still alive, if he had siblings, and even his likes and dislikes.

Nathaniel's reticence bothered her. Why, she could not say. If he was not willing to tell her, she should not pry. Perhaps he was a naturally reticent man, and she was refining too much on what she had implied the day they met

— that all convicts, by definition, were wicked, evil people. If Nathaniel's parents were convicts, it was natural that he would have been offended. Ella knew she would have been, had she been in Nathaniel's shoes.

And, she reminded herself, Nathaniel was a journalist, a most respectable profession. Not to mention his qualities of kindness and generosity, as shown towards herself. None of that would have been possible if he had been brought up in an atmosphere of depravity, Ella decided.

Who knew what circumstances had led to Nathaniel's parents being transported? And had Nathaniel not stepped in and saved her, she herself might have been forced to crime herself in order to survive.

Ella resolved to be less judgmental, and to simply concentrate on the work Nathaniel gave her. For some reason, she wanted him to think well of her, and indeed he praised her handwriting, telling her his editor would be well pleased to receive neatly written articles for a change.

One evening, three weeks later, Nathaniel dropped a bombshell. 'In a few days I shall be travelling to Ballarat, Miss Matthews. My editor wants me to report on the latest developments there.'

'Ballarat!' Ella gazed at him excitedly, eyes suddenly alight with hope.

'Yes, I most definitely will ask about your brother.' Nathaniel smiled kindly at her. 'If I hear anything at all, I will write to you immediately.'

'I want to go with you.' Ella astonished herself with her boldness, but she looked at Nathaniel unwaveringly.

'I'm sorry, Miss Matthews, but the answer is no.' Nathaniel shook his head. 'I'll speak to Tingley and tell him that you are to stay here for as long as necessary. I'll give him a stern warning that if he cheats you or threatens you with the streets, he'll have me to deal with when I return.'

Ella remained adamant. 'Mr Lake, I want to go with you. Christopher is the only family I have. I worry constantly about him.'

'I know you do, but you've read my articles. Life is hard on the goldfields — and it's almost summer. In a few weeks it will be hot, searingly hot, the like of which you have never experienced in England. The goldfields are dirty and disease-ridden. There is drunkenness, violence, and crime.' Nathaniel again shook his head. 'No. I cannot, in all conscience, take you there.'

'Why should it be any more difficult for me than for you? And don't you dare say it is because I'm a woman! I know there are many women on the goldfields. Christopher himself told me so in his letters, and you yourself have written about them in your reports. If they can cope, so can I.'

'I cannot take you because I feel a duty of care towards you. I on the other hand, a single man with no family, have only myself to worry about.'

Ella's heart leapt on hearing this. Ruthlessly ignoring it, she said stoutly, 'I too am single, Mr Lake, and my only brother is there in the goldfields.'

'Miss Matthews, I'll ask after your brother, but let me be blunt. I don't hold out much hope. There are thousands of men out there — thousands. And Matthews is not an uncommon name; I'll no doubt be directed to many diggers of that name, none of whom will be your brother. He may not even be in Ballarat — he may have moved elsewhere.'

Ella nodded. 'He may have, but I'm sure he would have written to tell me so if he had. No — I feel Christopher is still in Ballarat.'

'A letter may have gone astray, but let's suppose he is still there. There is another problem: I do not know what Christopher looks like. I could walk right past him and never know he was your brother.'

'Exactly.' Ella seized on this point. 'It

makes sense if I accompany you. I know my own brother — and rest assured, I have no illusions about the difficulties I will face on the diggings. I'm not expecting a pleasure trip. Please, Mr Lake. Christopher is my only family.'

After a lengthy pause, Nathaniel gave a deep sigh. 'Very well, Miss Matthews. I shall take you with me. I hope you won't regret it.'

'I am more hardy than I look.' Yet Ella felt a little ripple of apprehension. She hoped her words proved to be true. She made a silent vow that she would not complain, no matter what hardships lay before her, and give Nathaniel no cause to regret taking her.

'I must warn you to prepare yourself for disappointment. Your brother may very well be in Ballarat and we may never find him.' Nathaniel gestured towards Ella's neatly arranged hair. 'I assume his colouring is similar to yours? Brown hair, hazel eyes?'

'Our hair is almost the same shade of brown, yes. But Christopher's eyes are not the same colour as mine. They are different, very different.' Ella paused for effect, smiling smugly. 'I think, even amongst the thousands of men working on the goldfields, Mr Lake, somebody would remember if they had seen a man with one green eye and one blue, wouldn't you say?'

3

The journey to Ballarat took just over a week. And what a journey it was! Ella had travelled by train several times in her life; her very first train trip was taken when she had travelled to take up the post with Mrs Pugh, and she had, during her time as companion, accompanied her employer when she visited various relatives and friends. When Ella had resigned from her post, she had again taken the train back to London, then another to Southampton in order to board the ship that would take her to Australia.

Now she was travelling to Ballarat in a dray, a type of covered wagon. If Nathaniel still entertained doubts about her decision, she at least gained his approbation in the matter of her luggage. Ella did not feel the need to explain that her baggage was so sparse because it was all she possessed!

Her small, battered, yet hard-wearing trunk and holdall bag were easy to store in the dray. Nathaniel was also travelling with the minimum of baggage, leaving his heavier and bulkier possessions in the care of Mr Tingley.

Their travelling companions were an entirely different matter. Ella and Nathaniel had joined a party going to Ballarat, all sharing the dray. After the driver had packed their possessions under the seats, he turned to regard stonily the items the other passengers presented hopefully to him, immediately announcing his refusal to transport two massive trunks, a pile of books and, to Ella's utter amazement, a piano.

The owner of the piano and books, a finely dressed young gentleman with a haughty air, was insistent. 'I cannot leave these, my man. I paid a fortune for them, as I know I shall need them to while away the evenings.'

Ella heard Nathaniel, standing beside

her, smother a laugh. Indeed, she herself was having difficulty not showing her amusement. Surely the young gentleman could see the dray could not possibly carry the huge pile of books, let alone a piano? Did he know nothing about the goldfields?

But the driver was used to dealing with unreasonable passengers. He simply refused to let the young gentleman board until he reduced his luggage. If he did not, the driver announced, young sir could walk to Ballarat, carrying his piano on his back for all he cared.

'But what shall I do with it all? I cannot take it back to the hotel!' The young gentleman protested.

The driver shrugged. 'Have a sale.'

The young man goggled. 'What the devil are you talking about?'

'Just what I said, sir. Call out, 'Sale'. Somebody will come along and buy it all, you mark my words.'

Ella, who had been wondering herself what would happen to the piano and books, was further amazed that within twenty minutes they were sold.

As the piano was borne away by a brawny gentleman who did not look particularly musical — but whom Ella suspected was eager to spend some of his gold — Ella turned to Nathaniel. She could hardly believe what she had just witnessed.

'I don't know what amazes me more, that people buy things straight off the street, or the fact that they want to take a piano to the goldfields!' Ella shook her head. 'A piano! Really!'

The driver heard her. 'It's because gold makes fools of people, miss.' He flicked the reins and the horses moved forward. 'Addles their brains!'

Ella wondered how the young gentleman would fare; indeed, how she herself would fare, with the hardships she knew lay ahead. She was voyaging into the unknown, but unlike the young gentleman — who was clearly the adventuring type that Nathaniel had spoken of — she did not expect an easy time.

Nathaniel, ever the journalist, was already taking notes. Ella wondered if the piano man would feature in his next article. Judging by the smile on Nathaniel's face, Ella suspected he would!

Their travelling companions included a young German couple who spoke little English and kept themselves to themselves, and another couple Ella took to be Londoners, judging by their accents. While the husband was calm, his wife shrieked loudly every time the dray made a sudden stop or dipped sideways on the track, which unfortunately was often. The fine young gentleman, whom Ella discovered was the younger son of a Norfolk baronet, kept up a litany of complaints.

The dray had a thick canvas roof, enough to shade them from the worst of the sun's rays, but it did nothing to lessen the heat. The horses' feet threw up clouds of dirt, coating everyone and everything in a layer of dust. The young gentleman complained even more as his clothes were ruined.

Ella wondered what her companions made of her and Nathaniel. They seemed to assume that they were man and wife, and neither Ella nor Nathaniel disabused them of the notion.

The nights sleeping under the stars were the best part of the journey for Ella, when she could put a distance between herself and her travelling companions, and rest the aches and pains she had accumulated that day.

On the second night, as Ella lay staring up at the star-studded sky, two possums snarled at each other in a nearby gum tree.

'If I had a gun, I'd shoot those things,' loudly declared the Norfolk baronet's son. Ella was glad he did not. He'd said the same thing when some kangaroos had suddenly hopped across the track in front of them, making the driver pull to a stop quickly, and when a koala was spotted fast asleep in a eucalyptus tree.

Ella would be glad to part company

with that particular gentleman! There seemed to be nothing about Australia that pleased or interested him.

For her part, she found the journey an incredible experience. The sight of the countryside and strange-looking animals, Ella found, diminished considerably the discomforts of the journey.

★ ★ ★

When the dray finally stopped at the outskirts of the Ballarat goldfields, Ella drew her shawl around her shoulders in an unconsciously protective motion and stared at the panorama that lay before her.

The sight that met her eyes was as different from the soft green fields of England as it was possible to be, and reinforced yet again the vastly different turn her life had taken — but one, she reminded herself harshly, that she herself had willingly undertaken.

Her first sight of the goldfields would stay with Ella for the rest of her life.

The first thing that struck her was the number of tents she saw, rows and rows of them, but the ambience here was the complete opposite of Canvas Town. Where Canvas Town held hopelessness and despair, here in Ballarat it was activity and purpose.

Nathaniel had not exaggerated; there were thousands of people. Of the vast multitude most were men, but there were a great number of women and children too. All of them seemed to be moving, intent on their tasks — making the goldfields seem, from their vantage point, an endless sea of motion.

The creek that flowed down the middle of the goldfields was lined with diggers. Most of them appeared to be rocking a contraption that resembled a cradle, into which their companions poured buckets of water. Others lined the banks, swirling water in large tin pans. There was not a tree to be seen, nor even a blade of grass. All had been cleared away in the ever-encroaching search for gold.

'Well, here we are, at last,' their driver announced, gesturing at the unlovely scene with his whip. 'I wish you luck. Believe me, you'll need it!'

Ella saw that, with the exception of Nathaniel, everyone was deeply shocked. She had no doubt that her own expression was mirroring that shock. The fine young gentleman looked frankly appalled. His finely tailored clothes, now sadly rumpled, dusty and sweat-stained, would not last much longer, living in this environment, Ella thought.

The travellers, still in silent shock, collected their luggage and parted ways, neglecting to even wish each other good luck.

Ella stood by her bag, not quite knowing what to do next. Nathaniel fetched her trunk as well as his own from the dray, indicating that Ella take the carry bags over her shoulder. She followed Nathaniel down the well trodden path that led to the camps.

Ella suddenly stopped. 'Mr Lake,' she

said hesitantly. 'Where exactly are we going?'

'I thought, first of all, we'd ask around for your brother,' Nathaniel replied. 'We may be lucky enough to discover where he is today, although it's unlikely. If we don't find him, we'll find somewhere to stay, at least for tonight. Someone might put us up. Or we can purchase a canvas tent from one of the stores, so we'll have our own shelter.

'Now, stay close to me, Miss Matthews, and watch your step. I don't want you falling down an open mineshaft!'

Ella carefully followed in Nathaniel's footsteps, duly stepping around tent pegs, discarded shovels and picks, and keeping a wary eye open for mineshafts. She was also careful to avoid what Nathaniel called slag piles, the dirt and clay that was carried up from the mines and tossed beside mineshafts. Some of them were the size of small mountains.

Almost every nationality on earth

seemed to have converged upon Ballarat. As well as English spoken in a variety of accents, including the twang of Americans, Ella recognised French and German, but there were other languages she did not recognise. There were people from the Mediterranean and dark-skinned people from she could not guess where. To her astonishment, there was even a contingent of Chinese people.

No matter what their nationality, all the men had taken on a similarity. They wore big slouch hats to protect their faces from the sun, moleskin trousers and cotton shirts. Almost all had full beards, making them almost indistinguishable from one another.

Whenever they passed a group of English-speaking diggers, Nathaniel asked if anyone knew a Christopher Matthews, or had seen a tall, brown haired man with odd-coloured eyes.

Always the answer was 'No.'

As the afternoon wore on, Ella became more despondent. Now that

44

she was here on the goldfields, she wondered if she would ever find Christopher. When Nathaniel asked if she would like a rest, Ella readily agreed and they stopped beside a tent that was serving as a water store.

Nathaniel passed her a tin cup filled to the brim with clean water and Ella drank gratefully. She asked the question that had been bothering her. 'It's nearly evening, Mr Lake. What happens if . . . '

'There's still time to buy a canvas tent from one of the stores. We'll find a space wherever we can pitch it, although it will be cramped.' He gave her a level look. 'This is not the time to observe the niceties, Miss Matthews.'

Ella knew perfectly well what Nathaniel was referring to. Men and women, by necessity, were forced to live in close proximity. She would have no other choice than to share a tent with Nathaniel. She had been half expecting it, and now on closer inspection of the goldfields, all remaining doubts were wiped from her mind.

On their journey from Melbourne, they had been careful to keep a distance from each other when they slept. Here, space was at a premium. It would not be possible to sleep apart.

Yet the idea of sleeping in the close confines of a tent with Nathaniel made Ella jittery. She felt a hot blush sweeping over her, from her toes to her face. Hastily, she dropped her head, hoping Nathaniel had not noticed.

Stop being ridiculous, she chided herself. She had been expecting something like this. In the fullness of time, she would no doubt face worse privations. She couldn't afford to indulge in a fit of the vapours!

After their rest, they resumed their search. It was fruitless. No one had heard of a Christopher Matthews, nor had anyone seen an odd-eyed man about the diggings.

Ella's heart sank. She was beginning to wonder if she would recognise her own brother among these thousands of bearded, purposeful men.

4

As evening drew near, Ella and Nathaniel stopped at another store tent, this time to purchase some bread. Sitting on wooden crates set outside the tent, they munched silently. The sun was setting, casting a gentle orange glow over the dry, dusty goldfields. The day was drawing to a close. Weary diggers took up their picks and shovels and trudged back to their tents.

'There's nothing more we can do today,' Nathaniel announced. 'We'd best find somewhere to sleep before it gets too dark.'

Ella stood up. Every bone and muscle in her body seemed to be aching, and she was so tired that she was almost swaying on her feet.

In the event, it was surprisingly easy to find somewhere to sleep. A digger, recognising Nathaniel from his last visit to Ballarat, offered them the hospitality of his camp.

'You and your wife will have the tent, of course,' Giles Hammond told them. 'I'm happy enough sleeping under the stars. Done it before, and I'll do it again before too long.'

'Miss Matthews is not my wife,' Nathaniel hastily explained. 'She's travelled with me to Ballarat to search for her brother. I'll sleep outside, too.'

Mr Hammond, on hearing this, looked slightly disapproving, a somewhat incongruous expression given his bearded dishevelment and unwashed appearance. 'Miss Matthews . . . ' He harrumphed, then turned to Ella. 'I see. What is your brother's name, miss? Perhaps I know him.'

Ella told him, and went on, 'If you don't know him, perhaps you may have noticed him. Christopher has unusual eyes — one green, one blue. Do you recall seeing such a man?'

Mr Hammond thought a moment, then shook his head. 'Can't say as I have, miss. Never met anyone called Matthews either, to my knowledge.'

Ella let out a tired sigh.

'We'll try again tomorrow, Miss Matthews. What we need is a good meal and a night's rest,' Nathaniel said.

After a meal of salted mutton washed down with a mug of tea, Giles Hammond showed Ella to his tent. The bed was nothing more than a pile of sacking on the floor, and none too clean, but Ella lay down with relief, using her shawl as a pillow and taking off only her shoes. The week's journey from Melbourne, combined with the fruitless search for Christopher had taken its toll, and despite her discomfort, she was soon asleep.

* * *

Ella woke early. Mr Hammond gave her a brief good morning, and told her breakfast would soon be ready.

Nathaniel was sitting by the camp

fire shaving, a small mirror balanced on his knees and a basin of soapy water by his feet.

'Waste of time, that,' Mr Hammond observed. 'Much easier to let your whiskers grow out. A beard saves you from getting sunburnt, too.'

'Maybe so, but I prefer to be clean-shaven.' Nathaniel patted his face dry with a piece of linen. 'After all, I am a respectable journalist!'

Mr Hammond had a bowl of water ready for Ella to wash her face and hands and, ablutions complete, their host handed them each a plate containing thick slices of stringy-looking meat. Ella sensed they had had the same meat the night before, but in the unforgiving morning light, the meal looked distinctly unappealing.

'Yes, mutton again,' Nathaniel said in a low voice, confirming Ella's suspicions. 'The staple of the goldfields! You will be eating a lot of it.'

Ella chewed the meat slowly. The mutton was very salty, and although it was unappetising, it was filling. After a mug of tea, she and Nathaniel bade farewell to Giles Hammond and they were on their way.

Again and again, Nathaniel asked the same question and received the same answer — no one knew a Christopher Matthews, nor had they seen an odd-eyed man on the diggings.

They stopped only at midday for a meal and a rest, and before Ella knew it, another day was drawing to a close.

They were sitting outside a water store when a weary digger passed them, his pick slung over his shoulder.

'Hello, Jim.' Nathaniel hailed him. 'How are things?'

'Ah, Nat, back again? They're still interested up in Sydney, then?'

'They're still interested, Jim,' Nathaniel confirmed. 'The whole world is.'

Jim only nodded at this and said, 'Well, can't say as it's been so good for me lately. I've been thinking about returning to Melbourne, find myself some honest work.' His face took on a glum expression at the very idea. 'I'll see what happens in another week or so.'

Before Jim could further expound on his ill fortune, Ella spoke. 'Have you heard of a man called Christopher Matthews?'

Jim stared at her for a moment, and then scratched his beard. He didn't seem offended at her interrupting, nor did he evince any curiosity as to who she was. 'Can't say that I have, miss. Most of us just call each other 'mate.''

'He's tall, has brown hair, and has odd-coloured eyes,' Ella prompted. 'One blue, one green.'

Jim perked up. 'Ah . . . now you mention it, miss, I think I did see a fellow with eyes like that.'

Ella fought to hide her impatience as Jim frowned and scratched his beard again. 'Or was it one green, one brown? No, one was definitely blue.' He nodded decisively. 'Yes, blue. Now, where did I see him?'

Again his brow furrowed in thought,

scratching his beard ever more vigorously while he searched his memories. Ella bit her tongue. Hectoring Jim wouldn't help.

After what seemed an age, Jim nodded again. 'Yes, I definitely remember seeing a fellow with odd eyes. A few weeks ago I was talking to Patrick Milligan. There was a fellow with him, not that I spoke to him, but I do remember his eyes. As you would. They catches the attention, like.'

Ella clapped her hands as she turned to face Nathaniel. 'It's Christopher. It has to be!' With renewed energy she leaped to her feet, seizing the bags.

Nathaniel put his hand on her arm to stay her.

'Patrick Milligan, you say?' he asked. 'Where may we find his camp?'

As Jim gave directions, Ella tried to calm herself. Of course it wouldn't do to go haring off across the goldfields without asking for directions! She really must learn to be sensible.

As they set off in the direction Jim

indicated, Nathaniel urged caution. 'This man may not be your brother, Miss Matthews. With these numbers of people on the diggings, it isn't inconceivable that there could be more than one man with one blue eye and one green. Or Jim might be mistaken. The man he saw could have one green eye and one brown, as he initially said.'

'And Jim might *not* be mistaken.'

'Well, let's hope you're right.' Nathaniel didn't sound hopeful, but now that there was a possibility of meeting her brother, Ella's hopes rose.

Even though they carefully followed Jim's directions, they got lost twice before finally finding the Milligan camp. Patrick, it appeared, had a wife called Deirdre. They were well known, and Patrick, at least, seemed to be well liked. Ella wondered what Deirdre was like, and how Christopher had met them. *If it is Christopher*, she reminded herself. She didn't dare think about what she would do if this odd-eyed man turned out to be a stranger.

As they reached the Milligan camp, Ella saw a strikingly pretty young woman tending a camp fire. Her long dark hair was tied back simply with a ribbon, and she was wearing a skirt and a cotton blouse, both rather grubby and worn. As Nathaniel and Ella approached her, she rose to her feet, her rich blue eyes regarding them with suspicion.

Nathaniel took off his hat and nodded a greeting. 'Good evening. I believe you're Mrs Milligan?' The young woman nodded. 'We're searching for Christopher Matthews. We've been told that a man with odd-coloured eyes is a member of your party.'

'You're correct.' Deirdre spoke with a marked Irish accent. 'Your Christopher Matthews joined my husband and me just over three months ago. What do you want with him?'

'Christopher's my brother,' Ella burst in eagerly. 'Is he here?'

'No, he's not.'

Ella's heart sank.

Deirdre continued with a smirk, 'I mean he's not here now. He's still down at the mine with Pat, but I'm expecting them back any minute.'

Nathaniel said kindly, 'This lady is Ella Matthews, Christopher's sister. She's travelled all the way from England to find him.'

'Has she indeed? How nice. I hope you had a pleasant trip, and haven't been too distressed by what you've seen of the diggings. What do you intend to do now you're here, Miss Matthews?'

Deirdre's voice contained a hint of a sneer. She looked Ella up and down, regarding her as if Ella had stepped from a coach and four dressed in a ball gown instead of workaday clothes — not dissimilar to what Deirdre herself was wearing, although of slightly better quality. And slightly cleaner.

'I thought I would stay with my brother.' That's if Deirdre let her, Ella thought. The Irish girl's manner was far from hospitable.

'This isn't a London drawing room,

Miss Matthews. I have enough to do without waiting on you hand and foot,' Deirdre began.

'Dee, what's going on here?' A man, who could be none other Patrick Milligan himself, walked up to them, looking utterly exhausted. He was some years older than his wife, whom Ella thought was perhaps slightly younger than herself.

'These two English are looking for Christopher Matthews.'

A man was following close behind Patrick. Ella looked at him uncertainly before recognition dawned. Yes, it was definitely her brother!

'Christopher!' Ella began. The expression on her brother's face cut off the rest of her greeting. He looked far from pleased to see her.

'Ella? What the devil are you doing here?' he snapped.

Like Patrick Milligan, Ella could see that Christopher was almost dropping with exhaustion. Yet his annoyance was evident. He was barely recognisable as the dapper man-about-town Ella had known in England.

Christopher was almost indistinguishable from all the other diggers. He was bearded, and wore a red shirt and moleskin trousers. He was very dirty, very sweaty, sunburned, and looked very, very tired. The only thing about him that was still recognisable were his odd-coloured eyes.

'I asked you a question, Ella. What exactly do you think you are doing here?' Christopher repeated, as Ella continued to stare dumbly at him.

'Your sister has been worrying about you.' It was Nathaniel who answered Christopher's irritable question. 'You've neglected to write to her. You might also be interested to know, sir, that whilst she was in Melbourne, she was running out of money.'

He sounded almost as angry as Christopher. Ella looked at Nathaniel in some surprise.

'And who the devil are you?' Christopher was now almost snarling.

Ella broke in. 'This is Mr Lake, Christopher. He helped me in Melbourne. I hadn't heard from you. I've been so worried. Mr Lake is a journalist, so — '

Christopher waved her explanation aside. 'I didn't want you travelling out here, Ella! This is no place for you. You were to stay in Melbourne until I fetched you. You cannot know how difficult life can be here, and I knew you would be safe at the hotel. I specifically told Tingley that you were to . . . '

Now it was Ella's turn to become irritated. 'As Mr Lake has just told you, Christopher, I was running out of money! It was only a matter of time before Mr Tingley cast me out into the street.'

Christopher looked shocked. 'He would not do that! He assured me he would look after you until I came for you.'

Nathaniel made a sound suspiciously like a snort.

Ella ignored him, and continued speaking. 'I did manage for a while, but you may not be aware of how difficult things have become in Melbourne. I was in danger of losing my room, and if it wasn't for Mr Lake, I would have ended up in Canvas Town. I knew no one, had no work and with things the way they are, no prospect of obtaining any. And you did not write. I've been sick with worry. I didn't know whether you were ill or . . . or . . . ' Her voice broke. 'I had to discover whether you were all right.'

The fear in her voice was palpable. Christopher looked shamefaced.

'I'm sorry, Ella. I had no idea. I know I should have written, and I've been meaning to, but I've been so busy the past few months. But you could have written to me telling me you were running out of money.'

'Send a letter addressed to Christopher Matthews, Ballarat?' Ella retorted with scorn. 'There are probably several other men here that bears your name.

Besides, I couldn't even be sure you were still in Ballarat.'

Pat Milligan broke in, playing peacemaker. 'Look, we're all very tired and very hungry — and this conversation is doing none of us any good. Enough. Your sister is here now, Matthews, and that's that.' He turned to his wife. 'Do we have enough food for our guests, Dee?'

'Yes,' Deirdre answered, although she still looked disgruntled. 'I managed to find some good mutton today, and we've still some tea left. I've also made a damper. There's enough to go around.'

'Excellent! I'm sure we'll all feel better after a meal and a night's rest.'

Deirdre was still grumpy. 'And where are these two to sleep, Pat?'

'They can share Christopher's tent,' Pat decided. 'Lucky it's a big one. I'm sure our guests are capable of looking after themselves — they managed to find us, so they're hardly incompetent! Serve the meal, Dee, and then we'll go to bed. Tomorrow is soon enough to discuss what's to be done.'

Christopher fetched two crates from his tent to join the ones already set around the fire. Ella and Nathaniel sat down.

Deirdre served the meal, which was surprisingly good, if plain. Damper, Ella discovered, was a type of unleavened bread and although there was no butter to go with it, it was good and filling.

After his third cup of tea, Pat stood up. He rubbed his lower back. 'I'll bid you good night then, Miss Matthews, Mr Lake. We'll speak in the morning.' Deirdre went with her husband, casting another sour glance at them over her shoulder as she went.

'Don't mind Dee. She's had a rough time of it,' Christopher told them.

'How did you meet the Milligans, Christopher?' Ella wanted to know.

'By chance. They travelled here with another couple from Ireland, intending to work as a team. The other couple didn't take to the work — the wife refused to lift a finger, and the husband was little better — and they soon parted company. I arrived in Ballarat a week or so after the Milligans had been deserted by their companions. I'd been asking around if I could join a team. Pat welcomed me with open arms. You're more likely to find success if you work in a team, you see. It's a hard slog if you intend to dig for gold on your own, although some men do.'

'And have you had any success?' Nathaniel enquired.

Christopher shrugged. 'When I first started out, none at all, I have to admit! I soon regretted asking you to come out to join me, Ella, but when I learned my lesson it was too late to stop you. But I thought you would be safe in Melbourne.'

Ella put her hand over her brother's. 'I've managed. As you seem to be.'

'Yes.' After a pause, Christopher shook himself. 'We're managing. Pat and I found a little gold with the previous two mines we worked. Enough to keep ourselves fed, at any rate. But Pat thinks this shaft is the lucky one. It's the third we've bought, so here's hoping, third time lucky!' He lifted his hand, crossing his fingers.

'Do you work with the Milligans then, Christopher?' Ella inquired. 'Pat seems nice, but Deirdre is . . . ' She trailed off searching for the right word.

'Prickly,' Christopher supplied. 'I think she would prefer it if I was Irish, but I pull my weight, so she tolerates my being English. Besides, out here the old feud between the Irish and English somehow seems irrelevant.' He stood up. 'Another busy day tomorrow, so we'll need our sleep.' He looked at Ella. 'I take it you are intending to stay? I can't spare the time to escort you back to Melbourne. Unless Lake here is . . . '

'I was travelling here anyway, and your sister was insistent she accompany me. I'm here for stories for my paper, but I can assure you I won't sit around writing while the rest of you work. I've been down mines before, so if you'll have me, I'll stay a while. If I'm any judge, Patrick Milligan will welcome our extra hands.'

Christopher nodded. 'Pat will indeed. His back troubles him, and I know he suffers more than he lets on.' He gave his sister a level look. 'So you mean to stay here?'

Ella nodded. 'I do.'

Christopher sighed, but made no further attempt to dissuade her. 'Well, I daresay Deirdre will welcome your help, although I doubt she'll ever say so!'

'I'll work hard, Christopher. Deirdre won't think me a fine lady this time tomorrow, I can promise you that.'

Christopher grinned. 'Yes, I suspect Madam Deirdre is in for a surprise!'

He led the way to his tent. Ella was pleasantly surprised when she stepped inside it. Pat hadn't exaggerated; four people could comfortably sleep in it, if they weren't too finicky about the lack of privacy or space, and Ella knew she couldn't afford to be. She had made her bed, as the saying went, and she would lie in it. As Christopher lit the lamp that hung from the centre pole, Ella studied that bed.

Christopher had clearly made it himself. It was an improvised stretcher made out of what looked like flour sacks nailed out on wooden poles, the four corners mounted on forked sticks hammered into the ground. A blanket covered it, and over that was a rug of fur — Ella presumed of possum or kangaroo. The pillow was another flour bag stuffed with rags. Neither bed nor pillow looked particularly comfortable, but it was an improvement on the bed she had slept in the night before.

The tent also contained two wooden crates that served as seat and table. There was a shovel propped in the corner. Christopher's travelling trunk, now looking sadly battered and worn compared to when Ella had last seen it, was pushed to the opposite side from the bed. Clothes hung from various hooks hammered into the poles holding up the tent. The floor was dirt, with only a single rush mat set beside the bed.

It was primitive in the extreme, and made Ella's tiny room at Mr Tingley's hotel seem palatial. But she welcomed it. It was shelter, and besides, she was so tired she was almost falling asleep on her feet.

'You'll have my bed, of course, Ella,' Christopher told her. 'Lake and I will make ourselves beds of bush feathers.'

The odd phrase jerked Ella back to wakefulness. 'Bush feathers?' she repeated in confusion.

'Gum leaves, Miss Matthews.' It was Nathaniel who answered her question. 'You make a pile of them on the floor, spread a blanket over them and there's your bed. It's not that uncomfortable, but the crackling sounds the leaves make every time you turn over can be somewhat annoying.'

'If you intend to stay, Lake, we'll have to get ourselves more possum rugs. There are some Aborigines nearby that make and sell them. We'll get some tomorrow.' Christopher turned to his sister. 'We'll need them. Although it's almost summer, the nights are still cool.'

The two men then left the tent. It was growing darker by the minute, and they still had the 'bush feathers' to collect.

Ella lay down on the bed. She took off her shoes, but then found she couldn't harness the energy needed to get undressed. She cautiously lay down. She was right; the bed was uncomfortable. She briefly wondered whether, tired as she was, she would be able to sleep at all but before she knew it her eyes had closed and she drifted into unconsciousness.

5

When Ella woke the following morning, it was to discover that someone had drawn the possum skin rug over her. She sat up, faintly embarrassed. She hoped it had been her brother who had done it. It was bad enough being forced to share a tent with two men — even if one of the men was her own brother — but somehow the thought that Nathaniel had drawn the rug over her was too intimate to contemplate.

She shook herself as she sat up. She would have to toughen up and put aside any lingering missishness if she was to live here on the goldfields! She should be thankful that someone was thoughtful enough to cover her with the rug, ensuring that she slept the night through and not been woken through being cold.

There was a small tin dish containing

clean water sitting on a crate, and a piece of linen for drying. As Ella cleaned and tidied herself as best she could, she wondered what the time was.

The men were probably long gone. She only hoped she hadn't overslept too long. It wouldn't bode so well for her future relations with Deirdre.

'Ah, Lady Muck awakes,' Deirdre greeted her as Ella stepped from the tent. 'It's well past nine. If you intend joining us, miss, you get up early in the morning like the rest of us. Unless you've changed your mind and you'll be returning to Melbourne? No doubt it's been an awful shock to you, seeing how we live here.'

'Good morning, Mrs Milligan,' Ella said pleasantly, determined to be friendly. 'I apologise for oversleeping. I assure you that it won't happen tomorrow.'

'See that it doesn't,' Deirdre grunted. 'The men are already at the mine. You'll see them at midday when they come for their meal.'

Ella nodded, wondering how she was going to cope with spending the whole day in this frosty girl's company. Somehow she would have to; having made the decision to stay in Ballarat, she knew she had a lot to learn. Deirdre knew things she didn't. Ella wondered if they would ever be friends.

Sitting down on a wooden crate, she accepted the plate that Deirdre handed her. Mutton and damper again!

'Did Mr Lake say anything?' Ella enquired, taking a bite of the damper.

'No, only that he'll talk to you later. He did tell Pat and me that he's a journalist, and that you've been assisting him with his articles.' There was a brief spark of interest in Deirdre's blue eyes, so brief that Ella wondered if she had imagined it.

'I have,' Ella confirmed. She saw that spark again in Deirdre's eyes. She hadn't imagined it; Deirdre was interested. 'So I don't arrive here a complete ignoramus, Mrs Milligan. I know I don't have the experience you have, but

Mr Lake has told me a lot. I know it's not easy living on the goldfields, so I would appreciate it if you would share your knowledge. I'm eager to learn and willing to work.'

Deirdre unbent, just a little, but it was a start. 'Well, that's something. Sometimes everything gets too much, and by night time I'm so tired I want to sleep for a week.' She looked around her in disgust.

Ella suddenly realised that Deirdre loathed living on the goldfields, that she hated the dirt, the indifferent food, the unrelenting work — not to mention that she was probably in a constant state of anxiety over Pat, working miles underground where disaster could strike at any time.

Ella softened towards her. 'I'm no fine lady, Mrs Milligan. I've been earning my own living for a number of years, and although being a companion to an elderly lady is nothing like working on the goldfields, I am accustomed to doing things for myself.'

Deirdre's head was bent as she furiously poked at the fire. Her long dark hair was covering her face so Ella couldn't see her expression, but she rather imagined that if she had been able to, she would see that the girl had been fighting back tears.

Deirdre made a sound suspiciously like a sniff, then said, 'Well, finish your meal, Miss Matthews, and we'll get started. There's lots to do before the men return for their meal.'

Ella looked around her as she finished the last of her damper and mutton. In the bright morning light, the goldfields appeared even less appealing. Again she was struck by how dirty everything was — how hot, dry, brown and grey.

No wonder Deirdre hated it. Ella suspected that she would come to hate it as well, and she hadn't yet been here a week!

Finishing her meal, Ella stood up. 'Right — to work. Tell me what you want me to do, Mrs Milligan.'

'We need more provisions.' Deirdre covered the pot that Ella suspected was boiling yet more mutton for their midday meal. 'Things like flour and tea I usually buy in bulk and store in the tent. But meat's a different matter,' Deirdre went on. 'That has to be purchased daily, for obvious reasons. And you must be careful.' Her lecture continued as she led Ella to the store tents. 'Some vendors will try to cheat you by fobbing you off with bad meat. And keep an eye out for pickpockets. They'll make off with both your purchases and your money if you're not watchful. Keep your wits about you at all times, Miss Matthews.'

Ella couldn't help but be impressed with Deirdre's haggling skills and the way she managed to get the freshest produce at a reasonable price, even if they were still roughly double the prices in Melbourne. And as Ella knew all too well, Melbourne prices were high enough. Living in London was so cheap by comparison!

'Now, tea and coffee.' Deirdre suddenly seemed subdued. 'I hate it when I have to buy tea and coffee.'

'Why? Are they of poor quality?'

Deirdre looked grim. 'Quite the contrary; it is the finest tea and coffee to be found on the diggings. No, it isn't that. It's John Marwood, the merchant who owns the store. I don't like him and I don't trust him.'

'Why is that?'

'You'll see.' Deirdre's grim expression only intensified as they approached the store tent. The name 'John Marwood' and below that, 'Tea and coffee merchant' was painted in bright red letters on a board nailed over the counter that was set up at the front of the tent.

No one appeared to be about. Deirdre rapped her knuckles sharply on the wooden counter.

The canvas flap was immediately lifted aside and a man, who could be none other than John Marwood himself, appeared.

From what Deirdre had implied, Ella expected a dark and sinister-looking man, but John Marwood was the exact opposite.

In fact, if Ella had to describe him, she would have to confess that John Marwood was really the most nondescript creature she had ever seen.

Of medium height, he was neither fat nor thin. His skin was very pale, almost doughy, as though he rarely ventured out into the sunlight. His pale hair, neither blond nor brown but some mousey shade in between, was sparse. His beard was equally sparse, although in contrast to the unkempt diggers, who sported beards so bushy birds could nest in them, his was neatly trimmed. His eyes were of so pale a blue as to be almost colourless. Not a man one would give a second glance at, and Ella couldn't immediately fathom what it was about him that Deirdre objected to.

'Ah, Mrs Milligan! Always refreshing to be of service to a pretty young woman.' His unctuous tones made it clear to Ella why Deirdre disliked him.

Deirdre's expression didn't lighten at these silky words. 'The usual, thank you, Mr Marwood, and be quick about it. I don't have time to chat.'

Marwood put on a hurt expression. His glance slid to Ella, a spark of interest lighting his pale eyes. 'But surely you can spare a moment to introduce me to your charming companion?'

'This is Miss Matthews. Now, we are very busy, Mr Marwood, so if you wouldn't mind — '

'Miss Matthews? An unmarried lady?' To Ella's consternation, Marwood looked her up and down openly. She stepped back a pace to create a greater distance between them. 'A respectable unmarried lady! An uncommon sight indeed on the diggings! Matthews . . . I know that name.' John Marwood tapped the counter with perfectly manicured nails. 'You must be related to that man with the odd-coloured eyes. His name is Matthews.' He gave her a penetrating stare.

'My brother,' Ella supplied unwillingly after a moment. She felt as if John Marwood was reading her mind, trying to gauge all her secrets. No wonder Deirdre disliked this man so!

Marwood beamed, once again all amiability. 'How utterly charming! A family reunion.'

'Tea and coffee please, Mr Marwood,' Deirdre rapped out, to Ella's relief. 'We really must be on our way.'

'Of course.' He handed Deirdre two small packets, one containing tea leaves, the other ready-ground coffee. 'Please do call again,' he called as they left the store tent.

Deirdre grabbed Ella's arm in a painful grip and hurried her away.

'Do not, I beg you, encourage that man, Ella,' Deirdre said, using Ella's given name without seeming to realise it. Ella saw she was genuinely disturbed. 'The goldfields are full to bursting of all kinds of rogues and undesirables, but the greatest rogue of all is that man!'

'How can you be sure of that?'

'For one thing, I know he sells grog.'

'Grog?' Ella frowned.

'Alcohol,' Deirdre explained. 'Also known as sly grog, because the government has passed a law banning the sale and consumption of liquor on the goldfields.' She looked wry. 'Although you'll soon see that nobody takes any notice of that! But if it was only that, I could ignore it. All men drink, you can't stop them. But Marwood is a rogue of the worst order, and not only because I suspect he's an ex-convict. I wish there was somewhere else I could purchase my tea and coffee, but he's quashed all his competitors, one by one.'

Ella was uncomfortably reminded of her thoughts regarding Nathaniel's possible convict connections the day she had first met him.

'But surely, if John Marwood has served his sentence . . . '

Deirdre gave her a straight look. 'Once a rogue, always a rogue. I don't trust him.'

Neither did she, Ella was forced to admit. She realised that she too had taken John Marwood in dislike, and resolved to be as ready to deflect any friendly overtures from him as Deirdre was.

* * *

When they returned to the camp site, Deirdre helped Ella rearrange the tent she was sharing with her brother and Nathaniel. They partitioned the tent by stringing a rope down the middle and flinging over it two large blankets, so that Ella had, in effect, her own little room.

'I hope you're not the type to scream at the sight of spiders and insects, otherwise you'll be forever screaming,' Deirdre remarked, standing back to survey her handiwork. 'The ants and spiders out here are bigger than anything you've ever seen in England. Or Ireland,' she said feelingly. 'You can get a nasty bite if you're not careful.

Make sure you turn your boots upside down and give them a good shake before you put them on.'

Ella shuddered. 'And shake the bedding out too, I suppose.'

Deirdre grinned. 'Always. A thorough shake every morning — and evening too, just in case.'

It was now well past eleven. The men would soon come for their midday meal. Deirdre tossed four rashers of bacon into a frying pan and a delicious aroma filled the air.

'After lunch, I'll show you where I buy the mutton. For our dinner.' Deirdre shuddered. 'We have it nearly every day, for breakfast, lunch, and dinner. I swear, when Pat and I buy our farm, Ella, I'll never eat mutton again! Ever. Our sheep will be for wool.'

Ella turned over the bacon. 'You're going to buy a farm?'

'Yes.' For the first time, Deirdre looked enthusiastic. 'Victoria is good sheep country, Pat says. He did a lot of

reading and research before we jour-
neyed out here, and he believes we can
make a success of it, so that's what
we're going to do. We're staying on the
goldfields until we've earned enough
money to buy our stock and land.'

'I hope it won't be too long before
you're able to do so, Mrs Milligan.'

'Please call me Deirdre. And what are
your plans, Ella? I know your brother
has no intention of staying in Australia.
You'll go with him when he returns to
England, I expect.'

'Yes.' Ella took the frying pan off the
fire and tipped the bacon onto a plate.
She wondered why the thought of
returning home was suddenly depress-
ing. Not so long ago she had been
yearning to return! 'Christopher wants
financial independence. That has always
been his aim.'

'Nothing wrong with that,' Deirdre
allowed. 'Very sensible. And your friend
Mr Lake already has a job, so he'll be
returning to Sydney sooner or later.
Probably sooner; he has no real reason

to stay on once he has gathered enough material for his articles.'

'No.' Ella's mood became even more despondent. She was already aware that Nathaniel was here in Ballarat for his paper and that he would eventually return to Sydney, just as she herself would eventually return home to England with her brother. Why these facts should suddenly disturb her so much, Ella wasn't able to fathom.

She pushed them aside as she continued with her tasks. It was probably only anxiety. After all, her life had taken an unexpected turn; it was enough to unsettle and fluster anyone, let alone someone who had, until recently, been a mere companion living a very uneventful life.

The men arriving for their midday meal in a noisy bustle was a welcome distraction from Ella's confusing thoughts. Hot and tired, they were more than ready to eat. Deirdre served the meal, and then she went and sat herself at Pat's side.

'And how has your day been, Ella?' Nathaniel came to sit beside her. 'Are you ready to flee back to Melbourne yet?'

'Ask me that again in a week, Mr Lake.' Ella wondered whether Nathaniel realised he had used her name, yet it seemed natural that he do so. After all, they had spent so much time together these past weeks. However, Ella felt reticent in addressing Nathaniel equally informally. 'Deirdre's been keeping me busy. She's been very instructive.'

Nathaniel laughed. 'I'm sure she has. A most redoubtable young woman indeed. Pat's an extremely lucky man.' He gazed across at Deirdre where she sat very close to Pat.

Ella stared down at her plate. She knew she couldn't compete with Deirdre in looks. Even with her grubby clothes and lank, unwashed hair, the other girl was extremely attractive. No wonder Nathaniel couldn't help looking at her.

Ella shook herself. The sun must be

affecting her! It wasn't like her to be jealous, and yet for some reason she was. It seemed wrong to feel such an emotion, especially as she was beginning to like Deirdre. But she couldn't help wishing Nathaniel would stop looking at her.

As soon as the meal ended, the men headed straight back to the mine. Deirdre sighed as she collected the plates. 'Let's rinse these, and then we'll go and buy fresh mutton for our supper. We need more drinking water, too.'

By late afternoon, Ella was almost too tired to think. She had made three trips to the water vendor, and Deirdre had given her a lesson in making damper. It was the bread of the goldfields, made from flour, water, carbonate of soda and salt. Her loaves were now baking in an iron pot buried deep in the hot coals. They would be ready for breakfast.

Despite her exhaustion, Ella was pleased with her efforts.

After the evening meal, everyone relaxed. Pat lit a pipe, and arm in arm with Deirdre, set off for a stroll by the creek. Christopher muttered something about wanting a drink and sloped off into the darkness.

Nathaniel and Ella were left alone by the camp fire. Ella slowly sipped a mug of tea as she watched Nathaniel flick through his notebook. The once pristine white pages were now decidedly grubby.

Nathaniel frowned, squinting at his work by the light of the fire. He held the pages dangerously close to the flames in order to read them.

'I could write out your notes tomorrow,' Ella offered.

Nathaniel shook his head. 'Not any more, Ella. From now on you'll be far too busy, and far too exhausted, to be my amanuensis.'

'No more tired than you,' she argued.

Nathaniel closed the notebook. 'No. I'll write them out in my own time. My editor knows I'm in Ballarat and won't be expecting a work of calligraphy. He's dealt with my scrawl before. I'm sure he'll grumble and complain, but he'll decipher my handwriting in the end. I'll write them out as neatly as I can on Sundays, and send them by mail carrier to Melbourne on Monday morning.'

'I'll make a better job of it than you ever can,' Ella said stubbornly. 'You said so yourself.'

Nathaniel again shook his head. 'You say that now, Ella, but believe me, with the multitude of tasks you'll now have to complete, you'll barely have a moment to yourself. And when you do, you'll want to rest — and will need to rest.' He gave her a level look. 'Because you're definitely not fleeing to Melbourne, are you?'

Ella shook her head. 'No.'

'How long will you stay?'

Ella shrugged. 'That's up to Christopher.'

There was a silence, and Ella was disconcerted to see that Nathaniel was looking at her intently.

'Ella, have you ever thought that you could possibly . . . '

Nathaniel didn't complete his sentence. Pat and Deirdre had returned from their walk in a flurry. To Ella's surprise, the normally placid Pat seemed livid, an emotion she suspected was normally alien to him.

Pat stabbed his pipe in Nathaniel's direction, a visible sign of his agitation. 'I have something you can write for your paper, Lake. There's been another robbery. Dee and I just heard. It was the Richardson party this time. Mrs Richardson is beside herself. Everything she and her husband and sons have worked for has been stolen. Everything! It's an outrage!'

'I will certainly write about it, Pat. You can tell me about it in a moment.'

Pat nodded, and went to resume his seat by Deirdre.

'Robberies?' Ella asked as Nathaniel sharpened a pencil with his pocket knife. 'Deirdre mentioned thieves, pickpockets, and dishonest vendors. Does

Pat mean things are taken from tents?'

Nathaniel's face looked grim in the firelight. 'It's worse than that. I rather imagine what Pat means is robbery with violence. I very much fear poor Mrs Richardson has been menaced and her gold stolen. When we were down in the shaft today, Pat mentioned robberies. Empty tents have always been robbed, that's nothing new. The goldfields are full of opportunists. No, these particular robberies have taken a more violent turn. People have been attacked in their own tents, both men and women, their gold and valuables taken.' He looked at her. 'Be careful, Ella. There'll be times when you'll be left in camp by yourself. Be watchful.'

'Of course I will, Mr Lake.'

For a moment Ella thought that Nathaniel was about to say something else. He seemed to slightly shake himself. He looked over to where Pat and Deirdre were sitting. 'I wish there was a better method of hiding gold than burying it in tents.'

'The diggers bury their gold?' Ella was aghast. 'In the ground? But surely, if there are robberies . . . '

Nathaniel tapped Ella's nose with the blunt end of the pencil. 'What else can you do with it? You can hardly carry piles of gold around with you while you wait for the gold escort to arrive, so you bury it. Everybody knows that everybody buries their gold in or around their tents, so ergo, robbers and thieves know it too.'

Ella thought of all the unattended tents she herself had seen that day. Sometimes one man would be left in charge, or if a party contained them, the women were usually left. But nobody could be in their camps every minute of every day.

She and Deirdre had spent a considerable length of time away from theirs that very day. Anybody could have entered their tents, rifled through their baggage and taken whatever they wanted.

Ella thought of her small store of

money, which she was keeping in a small bag tied underneath her skirts, and felt faint. She had considered leaving it in her trunk until Deirdre had advised otherwise.

'If Pat keeps his gold in the ground, I suppose Christopher must, too,' she said tentatively.

'You're probably sleeping over it, Ella!' Nathaniel responded, smiling.

Until this moment, Ella hadn't given any thought as to where diggers stored their gold, but as Nathaniel said, where else could one store it until the arrival of the gold escort?

Yet it was definitely unnerving to think that she was probably sleeping atop her brother's pile of treasure!

6

As the next stages of Ella's new life unfolded, Nathaniel's words proved true. The days that followed were solid work; by evening Ella was exhausted, every muscle in her body aching. When she dropped into bed at night, she was asleep the moment her head touched the pillow.

Nathaniel wrote only on Sundays, the only day they did no physical work at the mine, even if other tasks still had to be completed. He would sit in the tent while he painstakingly wrote his articles on clean paper in his best handwriting, which was no match for Ella's neat copperplate! She wondered what Nathaniel's editor truly thought on receiving those scrawls again.

Deirdre was now leaving Ella in charge of the camp while she herself joined the men at the mineshaft. Ella would have liked to go too, but although she sensed that Deirdre now accepted her presence and had even begun to respect her, she remained protective of her privileged status as wife of Pat, the head of the 'Milligan party.'

Ella had also made friends with their neighbours, Mrs Barrett and Mrs Gibson. The Barretts were a married couple somewhere in their thirties, Ella guessed. The Gibson couple were the proud parents of four strapping boys. Although Ella was only on nodding acquaintance with their husbands — like all men on the diggings, they spent their days at their mines — she would occasionally join her neighbours for a mug of tea and a chat when they had their afternoon rest.

Ella looked forward to her afternoon breaks, as her days started early. The first task of the day was to purchase fresh water from the water vendor, setting it to boil to make it safe to drink. Then would begin the preparations for breakfast, which was simple but substantial — usually cold mutton, but sometimes varied with bacon and eggs, and occasionally butter, if it was available. On a few occasions, Ella even managed to purchase some apples, and one time — greatly daring at the expense — two oranges were shared amongst them. Luckily Pat didn't cavil, and he thanked her for her cleverness in finding them. Ella suspected that everyone enjoyed the oranges, despite the cost. They were certainly a delicious change from the ever-present mutton and damper!

Breakfast over, the men and Deirdre would make for the mineshaft, leaving Ella to tidy up and complete whatever tasks were necessary. After the dishes were done, bedding shaken out and left to air, Ella would make the round of the store tents for whatever provisions were required.

Ella was now growing used to these chores and to the rough ways of the goldfields and its men. Everybody was rough, including the store keepers, but none, however rough they were, were as objectionable as John Marwood. At least with the other men, what you saw was what you got, but there was just something about Marwood that was unlikeable. Deirdre was right. He was a rogue of the worst sort, although there was nothing you could put your finger on.

He was always scrupulously polite. Ella had never heard him use foul language or raise his voice, nor seen him drunk, yet whenever she had to visit his store, she would never linger and steadfastly refused to banter with him, keeping the transaction as short as possible.

One afternoon when Ella was alone at the camp, Deirdre having gone to join the men, she decided to tackle some mending. There was a large rent in one of Pat's shirts, and Ella was frowning over the problem when a shadow fell across her, blocking her light.

Startled, she looked up over her shoulder. It was John Marwood. Ella hastily rose to her feet.

'Miss Matthews!' Marwood gave her a little bow. 'I apologise for startling you, but when I saw you there, lost in your own little world, I just had to stop. I'm rather curious, you see. It's been a little while since I saw either you or the delightful Mrs Milligan. Surely by now you must have drunk all your tea!'

By sheer chance three days before, a pedlar selling tea had stopped by their camp and Ella, along with Mrs Gibson and Mrs Barrett, had bought a quantity from him. If the tea wasn't as good a quality as that stocked by John Marwood, Ella wasn't about to tell him so!

'We have enough for our present needs, thank you, Mr Marwood.'

'I do hope you haven't taken your custom elsewhere, Miss Matthews.' Marwood was smiling, but the smile didn't reach his eyes. Although he hadn't said anything overtly threatening, Ella sensed the underlying menace in his tones. 'I wouldn't want you to waste your pennies. Some of the stuff sold on the goldfields can be very bad. Even make you ill.'

'So I'm told. I thank you for your concern, Mr Marwood. Now, I must — '

'Your men are all away, I see. Busy at the mine, no doubt. And where is the charming Mrs Milligan? She hasn't left you here all alone, has she? Is she at the mine too? Is an extra pair of hands suddenly needed, perhaps?'

Some sixth sense warned Ella to be cautious with her answers. 'Not at all, Mr Marwood. Pat's back pains him and she prefers to be by his side.'

Marwood smiled his bland smile again. 'Ah, yes. I seem to recall that Milligan has a bad back. Poor fellow.' He sighed gustily. 'It's a precarious business, this gold digging. Much easier being a merchant. We're the winners in this madness!'

John Marwood certainly did appear to be a winner. Ella had already noticed how well he always dressed. His garments were finely made, and his leather boots, of a quality rarely seen on the goldfields, were obviously regularly polished, if now sadly dusty and with a hint of mud around the soles. A gold watch nestled in his pocket.

Ella found her eyes unwillingly drawn to it. 'Surely it's unwise to have your watch on display like that, Mr Marwood.'

'Oh, no one would dare try to steal from me, Miss Matthews.' Marwood patted his chest pocket. 'I never go anywhere without arms. It's a sad necessity in this lawless place. I hope Milligan has armed himself?' He raised a pale enquiring eyebrow.

Ella looked down at her feet, silently willing the man to go. 'I'm sure I wouldn't know, Mr Marwood. Well, I know you're a busy man and I have my tasks to complete, so I'll wish you good day.' So saying, Ella turned her back on him and sat down, picking up her sewing needle.

For a long moment, Marwood remained where he was. As Ella threaded her needle, she sensed his eyes boring into the back of her head. After what seemed an age, she heard him walk away, his boots crunching on the dirt.

She breathed a sigh of relief. The conversation had left her uneasy. Marwood had asked too many questions. Why?

'Are you all right, Ella?' Mrs Barrett's voice broke into her thoughts. Once again, Ella looked up. She gave her neighbour a pale smile. 'Yes, I am. John Marwood stopped by.'

'Yes, I saw him there and stayed in me tent.' Mrs Barrett frowned. 'He's always askin' questions that are none of his business. Nosy parker.'

'Yes, I've noticed.'

Not that she had anything to tell him, Ella assured herself. Every day the mineshaft was going deeper underground, but so far none of the buckets of soil hauled to the surface contained even a trace of gold.

Not that any of it was John Marwood's business!

Yet his curiosity bothered Ella, and again she wondered: Why was he so interested in them?

* * *

Although Sunday was a designated day of rest, there were still those necessary tasks that could not be put off. Making sure dishes and plates were cleaned was one of them, so after a leisurely breakfast, Ella gathered up the eating utensils to be washed and rinsed before the campsite could be overwhelmed by flies.

Pat and Deirdre had already left for Mass, which was held at a tent that served for Catholic services. Christopher stood up, stretched his arms over his head and yawned.

'Think I'll go and have another sleep until lunch,' he announced, and made for the tent.

Ella finished rinsing the plates in the bucket that was always kept near the camp fire. She set them aside to dry; they would be ready to use for their midday meal.

'There are Protestant services, if you should wish to go,' Nathaniel said. For a moment, Ella seriously considered it. She had always accompanied Mrs Pugh to church services, although her employer had always treated it as a social occasion rather than a religious one. Mrs Pugh would whisper constantly during the service, imparting her opinions on the women's clothes and hair, and after the service she would meet her cronies to catch up on the latest gossip and scandal. Ella, left to her own devices, usually took the opportunity to take a long walk around the countryside, making her own way home afterwards.

How she missed those walks! And

how long had it been since she had last been at a church service? Services had been held on the ship every Sunday by the chaplain, but since setting foot in Australia, Ella hadn't so much as looked in through a church door.

'Maybe not today,' she said eventually. Like everyone else, she was feeling somewhat lethargic, and the tent where she knew the Anglican services were held was some distance away. She reflected ruefully that Nathaniel was right; she certainly didn't feel up to re-writing his notes today!

'Would you perhaps like to accompany me for a stroll, then?' Nathaniel enquired. 'Just down to the creek and back. It won't be a picturesque outing, but it will do both of us good to get away from the camp.'

Ella hesitated. For some reason, her pulse had gone up a notch. Why, she couldn't fathom; it wasn't as if Nathaniel had asked her to dance!

Now, what had put that thought into her head? Dancing with Nathaniel!

Inwardly chiding herself, Ella nodded.

'Yes, I think a stroll would be perfect, Mr Lake.'

The day was pleasantly warm, enough to make one appreciate the caressing feel of sun on the skin without risk of burning. Ella and Nathaniel ambled slowly towards the creek. Today it was eerily silent. Cradles lay idle, shovels, buckets and pans lay where they had been cast down. A few men were there, sitting on fallen logs or lolling on the ground, all smoking pipes; others were sitting by the creek's edge, paddling their bare feet in the water.

Nathaniel didn't stop walking until they had left the men some distance behind. Only when they were alone did he stop. He turned away from her and gazed at the creek.

Ella stood beside him. She was acutely conscious of his tall form standing silently by her side. Cautiously she looked up at him.

He was still shaving regularly, although

today there was the hint of a shadow on his cheeks. Ella was unaccountably glad that Nathaniel made the effort to keep himself neat and tidy, despite the difficulties it presented. It pleased her that he wasn't letting himself become a bearded ruffian, as Christopher had already done!

As Nathaniel maintained his silence, Ella wondered what he was thinking about. She turned her own gaze to the creek. The sun glinting off the water was strong enough to hurt the eyes, and Ella adjusted her bonnet.

Suddenly Nathaniel broke the silence. 'It must call for a great deal of courage to travel so far on your own to a strange country,' he remarked.

Ella frowned as she retied the ribbon below her chin. 'I've never thought of myself as being particularly brave, Mr Lake, although if truth be told, I was apprehensive! Especially when I arrived in Melbourne, expecting to meet my brother, and he wasn't there. But the real reason I travelled here was because I felt stifled with Mrs Pugh. I think I even feared that I would spend the rest of my days with her in her gloomy old house. That was a prospect far more frightening, believe me!'

She shrugged deprecatingly before adding, 'I confess I liked the idea of travelling, too. I'd never been anywhere — not even to France — and now I've seen Rio de Janeiro and Cape Town. I've seen the sun rise over Table Mountain; it was so beautiful, I wish I had a talent for painting! I almost expired from the heat when we sailed through the tropics, and almost froze to death when we were becalmed in the Southern Ocean. I never expected to experience such things.'

Nathaniel smiled at her. 'It sounds as if you had quite an adventure! I'd like to travel one day. I've seen quite a lot of this country but I've never been to Europe.'

'Well, this country's certainly big enough.' Ella turned around, taking in her surroundings. 'The sense of space here is . . . well, it's almost as though there's nobody else in the world, even though I know the diggings are just over there.' She motioned in the direction of the camp site. 'Then miles and miles of space. And it's all so very different from England . . . '

Nathaniel laughed, making little crinkles appear at the corners of his eyes. 'And most of it no European has ever seen, although some intrepid souls are setting out on explorations.'

Ella thought about it. 'How exciting, yet terrifying. You could so easily become lost.'

'Indeed. I'm not sure whether I would be able to do something so audacious — or at least not without a great deal of preparation beforehand. Shall we sit over here?' Nathaniel gestured towards a great fallen gum tree and they sat down. Again they fell into a silence, listening to birds singing in the trees, insects chirping, and the sound of the sluggish water as it flowed by in the creek.

'I suppose exploration is necessary, if

Australia is to compete with Europe,' Ella said after a while.

'We will, given time. One only has to look at Sydney . . . '

'Oh, tell me about Sydney!' She turned to him.

'It's quite a town these days,' Nathaniel began with a smile. 'There are still a number of mud and daub huts from the earlier settlers, but they are gradually being demolished as new building takes place. All very busy and industrious! There are also shops. My parents run one.'

'What kind of shop?' Ella hardly dared to breathe; Nathaniel was about to disclose something about himself.

'An all-purpose general store is the best description I can give. They sell fabric, cutlery, books, stationery, furniture . . . so many things. Anything that isn't available in the shop can be ordered from England. It's quite an exciting day whenever a ship docks in the harbour with new supplies. The shop was a magical paradise for me and my brothers and sisters when we were growing up — so many hiding places, and playing with things we shouldn't have, imagining them on their long journey from England . . . ' Nathaniel smiled again. 'We had a happy childhood.'

Ella found herself smiling back.

'There are some good schools in Sydney too, and there are also balls, concerts, and theatre,' Nathaniel continued. 'We're not uncultured!'

Suddenly, without any warning and to Ella's great surprise, he brushed her cheek lightly with his finger. 'You're covered with dust, Ella.'

Ella's breath caught. She felt her eyes widen. Her heart missed a beat.

'Unavoidable, I'm afraid.' She hoped Nathaniel hadn't noticed the slight wobble in her voice. 'The track down here was very dusty. In fact, as I'm sure you've noticed, it's dusty everywhere. My face must be permanently covered in dust!'

'I'm sure mine is, too! We must all

look a sight.' Nathaniel stood up, holding out his hand to her. 'Come, Ella, it must be almost midday. Time for our meal.'

Ella took his hand, and Nathaniel tucked it into the crook of his elbow. She was very conscious of it; it was somehow an intimate gesture, yet quite proper. It wouldn't be out of place for a gentle stroll in a London park.

Nathaniel held her arm all the way back to the camp.

Only later did Ella realise that while Nathaniel had told her something of himself, it was still only a very little.

7

A week later the fortunes of the Milligan party took a new direction. Returning to the tent one evening, the men had an air of triumph about them. Pat, with a huge grin, almost skipped over to Ella. Taking her hands in his, he urged her to her feet.

'We've struck wash dirt, Miss Matthews!' he announced. 'This is our make-or-break stage. It'll be all hands on deck now, including yours. You'll work with us at the mine in the afternoons and turn your hand to cradling. I warn you, the wash dirt stage is harder than it looks.'

'Wash dirt?' Ella enquired. 'I think I've heard that expression before. That's a good sign, isn't it?'

'A very good sign,' Deirdre confirmed. For the first time, Ella thought she looked truly happy: 'It all but means we've struck gold, but not quite — although it does means more work! The dirt we bring up now has to be washed if we're to find the gold. Pat believes it's there!'

Although Ella had learned a lot about the ins and outs of gold mining, she remained ignorant of many things.

'You'll find out just how exhausting washing dirt is, Ella. It's hard work, and monotonous.' Deirdre grimaced at the thought. 'But it has to be done and we'll need your help.'

'Certainly, I'll do whatever you ask of me.' Ella returned their smiles, feeling that she was now truly a member of the Milligan team.

★ ★ ★

The following afternoon, instead of staying back at the camp, Ella accompanied Deirdre to the mineshaft. It was the first time she had been this close to it. Standing at the edge, she cautiously looked down.

Somewhere, far below in that darkness, Nathaniel and Christopher toiled away, filling bucket after bucket with earth, hoping against hope that one of the buckets would contain traces of gold.

How far down did it reach? All Ella could discern was darkness, although she could hear digging sounds.

Deirdre noticed her pensiveness.

'Yes, it's dangerous down there, but Pat's taken every precaution possible against accidents.' She sighed. 'I'll be so glad when this is over! I hate thinking of Pat working down in the dark, imagining what can happen . . . '

There was a sudden shout. 'Washing stuff!' Ella recognised it as Nathaniel's voice.

Pat, who today was not down the shaft but operating the windlass, immediately began winding the mechanism, slowly and carefully. Presently a bucket filled to the brim with dirt reached the surface.

As Deirdre brought the wheelbarrow

forward, Pat detached the bucket from the rope. He tipped the dirt into the wheelbarrow.

Deirdre, using a stick, spread the dirt out.

'I can't see any gold!' she wailed.

Ella couldn't see any golden sparkles either. It seemed incredible to contemplate that this pile of clayey-looking dirt could hold the key to a fortune.

'Well, we can't tell yet until it's been washed, lass,' Pat said, rubbing his lower back. 'Come along. Down to the creek we go!'

Trundling the wheelbarrow, the three of them went down to the creek where their cradle was waiting.

The muddy creek was all hurry and hubbub. Ella had been here a few times. The noise was incredible. The metallic rattle of gravel and stone being tossed about in hundreds of cradle hoppers as they were rocked to and fro produced an almighty din. Men had to shout at each other in order to be heard. At times, when the wind blew in the right direction, Ella could even hear the noise of it back at their camp. It sounded not unlike a low, rumbling thunder.

The other diggers around them were too busy with their own cradling to take any notice of the Milligan party as they set to work. As its name suggested, the big wooden contraption resembled a baby's cradle. Pat gently poured in the dirt into the cavity, while Deirdre spread it out over the bottom. Gently and slowly, Pat began pouring water over the dirt, then indicated to Ella that she should begin rocking. Taking the cradle's handles, she did so, moving slowly to the left and then to the right. It was hot and heavy work, and Ella soon felt perspiration break out on her forehead and down her neck. Deirdre all the while leaned over the cradle, poking at the dirt with the stick, casting out stones too big to pass through the perforated bottom, her face creased in concentration.

When all the water had passed through, washing away the dirt, only pebbles and small bits of rock were caught in the perforations. Deirdre checked carefully, then straightened up.

'No gold,' she said mournfully.

'Then it's back to the mine,' Pat said. Picking up the wheelbarrow handles, he led the way back to the mineshaft. Deirdre tugged on the rope. There was another shout — Christopher, this time — and presently another filled bucket was hauled up. And so the process was repeated.

Now that she knew what to do, Ella was left in charge of the cradle, her movements awkward now that Pat and Deirdre weren't there to help her. Every so often she stopped to spread the dirt with the stick as she had seen Deirdre do, and slowly pour water from the jug over the dirt. Then she would return to the handles and rock and rock and rock, until Deirdre and Pat returned, and the whole process was gone through again and again.

It certainly was monotonous work!

For two weeks it continued, and the

Milligan party were now more exhausted than ever. Every muscle in Ella's body screamed, and at times she found it difficult even to lift her arms. Nathaniel stopped taking his notebook down to the mine, and even ceased sending his reports on the mail carrier. Ella felt she had been cradling for years. Her time with Mrs Pugh seemed a lifetime ago.

Then one afternoon, as the long day was drawing to a close, everything changed.

Ella was rubbing her arms, wondering if they would ever recover, as Pat tipped in the last bucket of the day into the cradle. Tiredly, Deirdre poured water over it.

Once again Ella took the handles. The cradle rocked from one side to the other. As they watched, the last of the water seeped through the perforated bottom of the cradle.

What was left winked up at them in the sunlight.

It was the unmistakable glint of gold.

For a long moment, nobody said anything. Ella hardly dared to believe what she was seeing, but her eyes did not deceive her. There, caught up in the perforated bottom of the cradle, were tiny flecks of gold.

It was Deirdre who broke the silence first. 'Oh, Pat! We've done it! We've done it! Now we can leave this horrible, horrible place and buy our farm and never eat mutton again!' So saying she ripped off her bonnet and whooped with pleasure.

Pat retained his composure. Taking his knife from his belt, he carefully picked up the bits of gold with the tip and placed them on his palm. He examined them in the sunlight.

'Aye, it's gold, all right,' he said after a moment. He straightened up, wincing as he rubbed his lower back. 'Dee, go and fetch one of my little leather bags. You know where I keep them.'

Deirdre sped off, all her tiredness dissipated as if it had never been.

Pat gestured for Ella to resume the

cradling. 'There's still work for us to do, lass,' he said.

Ella cradled with renewed vigour. Pat fetched more water and gently poured it into the cradle, signalling her to stop occasionally so he could pick out the gold, dropping the pieces carefully into another bucket. It was building up into a neat little pile.

Ella wondered whether she was dreaming. She, a member of the Milligan party, was one of the 'lucky ones.' They were successful; they had found gold! She should be delirious with happiness.

And Ella was pleased, of course she was. Their find would mean that as soon as they had collected enough gold to ensure their financial security, Christopher could stop going down into the mineshaft, risking life and limb. They would be able to return to England and live a life of comfort.

Christopher had never made any secret of his desire to return home. He had confided to her on more than one occasion that he had had enough of life as a digger.

Ella did not share her brother's desire to return home. When she returned to England, she knew it would be a permanent return. She would have no reason to travel to Australia ever again.

Another thought struck her — Nathaniel was a professional journalist and already earning a steady income. Now that they had found their gold, there was no longer any reason for him to stay. He had his story. He could return to Sydney any time. Tomorrow, if he so wished.

For the first time, Ella wondered why Nathaniel had stayed with them. It was dangerous working in the mineshaft. She knew Pat had never asked him to stay, although he had welcomed Nathaniel's help.

So why had he stayed? He already had plenty to write about, and yet . . .

Ella's thoughts were interrupted by Deirdre's return. She skidded to a stop, holding up the leather bag, panting and laughing at the same time.

Pat took the bag and filled it with the gold. Some of the lumps were quite big. His hands shook as he weighed it. 'It's a good haul we have here. Too good! I'll be glad when this lot is sent off to Melbourne on the gold convoy!'

Ella silently agreed. Having all that gold around was distinctly unnerving, especially as there were still reports of robberies taking place. The sooner it was sent off on the gold convoy, the better.

As sundown approached, Christopher and Nathaniel emerged from the shaft and joined them at the creek. Just the expression on Pat's face was enough to tell the other men that they had found gold.

Christopher looked exhausted but delighted. 'I knew that bucket was the lucky one, even down there in the dark! How much do we have, Pat?'

When Pat told him, Christopher whistled and grinned ecstatically. 'We've struck it lucky — at last!'

Pat said, 'I have one more job for you, Matthews. Help me bury this so we can all enjoy a peaceful night's sleep! With all these robberies taking place, I want it out of sight as soon as possible.'

It was a tired, but happy group that returned to the camp that evening.

After the gold was safely buried, the Milligan party consumed their normal meal of damper and salted mutton.

Deirdre glared balefully at her portion. 'What I'd like, Pat, more than anything, is a long, hot bath with a cake of rose-scented soap. Then dinner at a fancy restaurant. Beef, lots of potatoes, and a bottle of fine red wine!'

Pat grinned back at her. 'We'll do that, Dee. We'll do all of that — depending on, of course, if there's any fancy restaurants still open in Melbourne . . . ' They continued their cheerful banter.

Nathaniel smiled at the couple and returned to his notebook, his pencil flying over the pages.

Christopher moved to sit beside Ella. He nodded towards the Milligans. 'Now there's a couple eager to make a new life here. And Nat, I expect, will be returning to Sydney soon.'

'No doubt.' Ella felt hollow. She couldn't help feeling envious of Pat and Deirdre, and the life they would build together here in Australia. It must be both a frightening and exciting prospect for them, to start a new life in a strange country, but they had the love and support of each other.

'It won't be long, Ella, before we too can enjoy our new life. I can hardly wait for the day I shake off the dust of this God-forsaken land and board the ship for home.' Christopher took Ella's hand and gave it a gentle squeeze.

'I haven't always been a good brother to you, but things will be different from now on, I promise.'

'I know they will be,' Ella said, and although she smiled back at Christopher, her heart was breaking. She had at last understood why the thought of returning to England was so distressing. The truth had dawned upon her that very afternoon.

Much as she loved her brother, she did not want to return to England with him. Like Pat and Deirdre, she wanted to stay in Australia.

It was not only that her adventures had changed her, making her unfit to return to life in England. Living on the goldfields had been difficult and, at times, unpleasant, yet she had revelled in it. She felt as if she had suddenly woken up after a long sleep to a life filled with new possibilities. The girl who had fetched and carried and read aloud to Mrs Pugh was no more.

And it was due to the man she had fallen in love with. Nathaniel Lake.

Nathaniel had given her no hint of his feelings towards her. He had treated her with respect at all times. They enjoyed each other's company and they worked well together, both in Melbourne and here in Ballarat.

And she, foolish creature that she

was, had, somewhere along the way, fallen in love with him. The shock of the realisation made her draw into herself, unwilling to talk further with her brother and unwittingly reveal her reluctance to return home. She couldn't bear for him to ask her probing questions just yet — not until she had come to terms with her feelings.

What could she do? Ella despaired. In a matter of weeks, or possibly even sooner if Christopher could arrange it, she would be boarding a ship bound for England ... taking her away from Nathaniel. And once back in England, she would never see him again.

8

Despite Pat's best endeavours to keep their find a secret, the news of the Milligan party's good fortune quickly spread. Reluctantly, yet with good grace at the urging of the other diggers, Pat agreed to host a celebration the following night, issuing an open invitation to anybody who cared to join them.

Christopher managed to find an amazing amount of grog — Ella did not dare ask from whom he had got it, suspecting that she wouldn't care for the answer — and the bottles were freely passed among their guests. It wasn't long before a number of the diggers began to slur their words and walk with a stagger.

Fortunately, not all of their guests became drunk and disorderly. Mr Barrett, to Ella's surprise, fetched his fiddle from his tent and began to play tunes, if not particularly tunefully! Soon there was laughter and dancing around the camp fire.

Ella and Deirdre were kept busy brewing tea and coffee for those who did not care for grog, when Ella saw Deirdre bristle.

'What are you doing here?' Deirdre asked rudely, looking over Ella's shoulder.

Ella spun around. John Marwood had arrived. At almost the same time, Mr Barrett stopped playing and glared balefully at Marwood.

'I don't recall inviting you,' Deirdre went on, her voice unfriendly. 'And I know Pat never would. Why are you here?'

Marwood smiled, seemingly not at all offended by Deirdre's rudeness. 'Now, is that any way to speak to a man who's only come to congratulate you and wish you well? I felt I had to come, after supplying Matthews with all those fine bottles of grog. To be sure, Mrs

Milligan, I count your party my best customers — as well as the one with the prettiest women.' His leering gaze took in both Deirdre and Ella.

His flattery did not please Deirdre. 'Be off with you!' she cried.

Marwood made no move to leave. He turned to Ella. 'Miss Matthews, I entreat you.' He lifted his hands, palms up. 'My intentions are good . . . '

'I think you had better leave.' Nathaniel suddenly appeared, carrying several empty mugs. 'We appreciate your good wishes, but our celebrations are for our fellow diggers only.'

John Marwood scowled. For a moment, Ella wondered if he would stand his ground and argue. The dancing had come to a standstill, and there were many unfriendly looks cast in his direction. Ella noticed that Mrs Gibson and Mrs Barrett, as well as a number of other women, young and old, were regarding John Marwood with positive dislike.

For a tense moment he remained

where he was. Then, without saying another word, he spun on his heel and left.

'That, I take it, is the infamous John Marwood,' Nathaniel stated.

'Yes. I wish Christopher had purchased that grog elsewhere,' Ella confirmed. A drunken digger brushed by her, making her stagger. Nathaniel reached out and caught her by the arms, steadying her. 'Or better still, had not purchased any at all!'

Nathaniel drew Ella away to stand by their tent. 'Indeed! He's quick to hear the news of our discovery — I wish he hadn't. I don't care for Marwood knowing our business. Where there's trouble on the goldfields, there Marwood is. Selling sly grog is only part of it.'

Ella started. 'You know him?'

'Not to speak to, but I've seen him on other goldfields — although he wasn't calling himself John Marwood then.'

'So Deirdre is right! She's always

saying he's a shady character.'

'I wonder if Marwood's aware he's now under observation by the police?' Nathaniel mused aloud.

'Is he? And how do you know that, Mr Lake?' Ella demanded, her curiosity aroused.

Nathaniel tapped the side of his nose. 'I'm a journalist, remember? I have my sources. And yes, Deirdre's quite correct. Marwood is definitely a shady character, and if he's as clever as he thinks he is, he should be making tracks. I'm surprised he's still here! Yet he appears rather settled here in Ballarat.'

Ella nodded. 'Yes, he does seem to like it here. Every time I go to his store, he's always telling me how well he's doing.'

Mr Barrett was now playing a waltz. Not very well, but it was definitely a waltz.

'Let's not spoil the rest of the evening discussing Marwood, Ella. Would you care to dance? I should warn you that

I'm a clumsy brute when dancing, but I'll be careful not to tread on your toes too heavily.'

Ella's heart thudded. A rush of pure joy flooded her. She ruthlessly suppressed it. Nathaniel was only asking her to dance; it wasn't a declaration of marriage! She must learn to be sensible. She was soon to return to England, and it would be prudent to remember that.

However, she would take what pleasure she could in the remaining weeks she had with Nathaniel.

'I should like to dance, Mr Lake,' Ella said in a calm voice, although her emotions were far from calm. 'Perhaps I should warn you, I too may be a little clumsy. I haven't waltzed since I was eighteen.'

'What a pair we'll make,' Nathaniel murmured with a wry smile, swinging her back towards the camp fire to join the other dancing couples.

Ella had attended a number of balls and dances in her younger years, held in crowded, stuffy ballrooms. At the time she had thought them heavenly. How naïve she had been!

In those days she had worn dancing slippers and beautiful gowns and had her hair styled in the latest fashion, listening to music played by the finest of musicians. But the memory of those occasions paled to nothing compared to dancing with Nathaniel in the open air, the smell of smoke and burning mutton redolent, the music indifferent, her clothing plain cotton.

Held in his arms, Ella was shielded from the worst of the bumps as other dancers, more inexpert and less sober than herself and Nathaniel, shuffled and romped past them. She couldn't remember enjoying a dance so much.

And it was probably the one and only dance she would ever have with Nathaniel. She would remember this night forever.

'You'll soon be returning to England,' Nathaniel said softly.

'Yes.' Ella wished that Nathaniel

hadn't brought up that particular topic. She wanted to treasure this moment, and not think of the bleak future that lay before her.

'You don't sound very enthusiastic.'

Ella shrugged. 'At this moment, England seems very far away, Mr Lake. It doesn't even seem like home any more. I shall miss Australia.' *And you,* she added silently. 'I'll even miss the goldfields, although there have been times when I've hated it. I know my time here has changed me. I'm not the same girl who fetched and carried for Mrs Pugh.'

'I doubt your Mrs Pugh would even recognise you, Ella. You're as brown as a nut, for one thing!'

Ella laughed. 'Thank you!'

'I'm paying you a compliment! The colour in your skin suits you. And you won't need to seek employment as a companion any more,' Nathaniel went on. 'You can do whatever you like. A brand new future awaits you. You must be looking forward to it.'

'Yes.' Ella's response was a bare whisper.

Nathaniel did not seem to notice Ella's distinct lack of enthusiasm. 'So what will you do?'

'I have no idea. I'll just have to wait and see.' Then, fearing that Nathaniel would question her further about her plans and discover her feelings for him, Ella said in a rush, 'And you'll be returning to Sydney soon.' It would be best to discover now when that would be, so she could better prepare herself.

'I will have to eventually. Not just yet, though. My task here isn't yet complete.' Suddenly Nathaniel stopped dancing. Taking her hand and tucking it in the crook of his elbow, he moved Ella away from the other dancers. Ella looked up at him in surprise, not expecting this.

Nathaniel turned her to face him. Holding her hands tightly in his, his thumbs gently caressing the palms, he looked at her, his expression earnest. 'Ella, there is something I want to ask you before . . . '

As had happened previously, Nathaniel's question was never asked. This time it was Christopher who interrupted them. Grabbing his sister by the waist, Christopher swung her away from Nathaniel and towards the firelight.

'Christopher, you're drunk!' Ella slapped at his hands in disgust, stepping away from him. Suddenly, she felt like crying at his intrusion. Her brother was a reminder of England, and she had wanted to spend the evening in Nathaniel's company.

'Of course I'm drunk, dear sister.' Christopher grabbed her hands again and spun her around the fire, not noticing his sister's mood. 'For good reason . . . we're going home to England, and I want to celebrate. Home, home! I can hardly wait.'

Yes, home. Ella told herself to remember that as she was twirled around by her brother. A man such as Nathaniel Lake was not for her. They came from different worlds. She should never have permitted herself to dream and hope otherwise . . . perhaps it was for the best that Nathaniel return to Sydney before she and Christopher left for Melbourne — the sooner the break occurred, the better.

9

Nathaniel gave no sign that he intended an imminent return to Sydney. On the contrary, the days following the celebration saw the Milligan party working harder than before, with Nathaniel doing more than his fair share.

Their cache of gold was growing steadily. Just a few more days' work, Pat told them, and then they could all start making arrangements to leave the goldfields. He was already in negotiations with a party who was interested in purchasing their mine.

They didn't dare leave the camp unattended now. Usually it was Deirdre or Ella who stayed behind, but on occasion, when Pat's back was particularly paining him, he would be the one to stay back.

'Bother!' Deirdre shook out what remained of the tea from the caddy. 'I wanted to brew some tea for Pat before I went to the mine. I thought we had more leaves than that.'

'I'll run and get some more,' Ella offered.

'Oh, Ella, would you?' Deirdre looked at her with real gratitude. 'I really don't feel up to dealing with any of Marwood's irritating remarks today.'

'Nor do I, but if we want tea, we have no choice. Do we have enough coffee?'

Deirdre checked the coffee tin. 'Yes. In fact, I do believe we have enough to see us out for the rest of the week. After that, it doesn't matter because we won't be here! It's just tea we need.'

'I'll get enough to last us a week then. After that, no more Marwood!'

'Hooray!' Deirdre cheered.

Ella's thoughts were in a jumble as she slowly walked to Marwood's store. Another week and the Milligan party would go their separate ways.

She would miss the Milligans, she mused, but perhaps she would write to Deirdre. Ella would be very interested to know how Deirdre and Pat were faring with their farm.

She wouldn't dare ask if she could write to Nathaniel, and it would be best not to. She and Nathaniel were but ships that passed in the night, and the sooner she accepted that fact, the better. Her life lay in England.

Ella was so deep in her thoughts that she was barely conscious that she had arrived at Marwood's store. She only returned to awareness of her surroundings when she was suddenly pushed aside by a tall, thickset man. He grunted rudely as he passed her. Ella had no more than a quick glance at him, but it was enough for her to notice his scar and the evil glint in his eyes. Never in her life had she seen such a villainous face!

'Oh!' She looked after him indignantly.

'Maskell, watch where you're going!' Marwood called out. 'You nearly knocked the lady over.'

Maskell only raised a beefy hand as

he continued on his way.

Marwood was all concern. 'I do hope my friend didn't hurt you, Miss Matthews?'

'He didn't,' Ella said shortly.

'Although — and I'm sure you'll forgive me for saying this — you really should look where you're going. But I suppose allowances should be made in your case. No doubt your mind is full of thoughts of all the pretty gowns and bonnets you're going to buy!'

'Our usual order of tea, please,' Ella said, making no response to Marwood's remarks. How dare he!

Marwood raised his almost nonexistent eyebrows. 'Tea? Is that all? Surely you can now afford to be a little more extravagant, Miss Matthews? How about something a little stronger, shall we say, so you can drink to your good fortune? I happen to have a bottle of the finest . . . '

'No, thank you, Mr Marwood. Tea will suffice.'

Ella completed the transaction and

turned away, her steps faster on the return journey. She mustn't let Marwood disturb her! After all, a week from now the Milligan party would leave the goldfields. She would never see John Marwood again.

Or Nathaniel, she reminded herself sadly, feeling the crushing weight of despair descending upon her once again.

★ ★ ★

Even the heavy workload was no balm to Ella's breaking heart.

Christopher's mood was the complete opposite. Ella couldn't remember when her brother had last been so jaunty. All he could talk about was London, and the fine life he and Ella would lead.

Ella furiously blinked away incipient tears as she rocked the cradle with unnecessary vigour. Hoping Deirdre would think her tearfulness was due to the glare of the late afternoon sun, she forced herself to concentrate on the task at hand.

The day had been a very warm one. It was almost summer and the days were getting longer and warmer. Soon it would be Christmas, a fact Ella found somewhat amazing as it fell in the middle of summer!

She wondered what Christmas in Sydney would be like. She now knew Nathaniel had parents and siblings, but did he have extended family? He might have nieces and nephews . . .

'Watch it, Ella!' Deirdre's voice brought Ella's attention back to what she was supposed to be doing. 'More of that water went over the side than into the cradle!' Tutting irritably, she poked the dirt around with the stick, extracting the last of the gold. Then she straightened up, her face wreathed in a smile. 'That's it for today! Tomorrow is the last day we work here.'

'Yes, the last day.' Ella's voice was hollow.

Deirdre looked sharply at her. 'What's

the matter, Ella?' Her brows rose. 'Have you been crying?'

'No, of course I haven't. I have no reason to cry . . . ' Despite herself, Ella felt fresh tears well in her eyes.

'Oh, what's brought this on?' Dropping her stick, Deirdre rushed to Ella's side. 'Have you hurt yourself?'

'No, I'm fine. It's just . . . '

'Ah, I think I know. It's Nat, isn't it?'

Ella felt her face flush. 'No, of course not . . . '

'Of course it is!' Deirdre contradicted. 'I do notice things, you know, and I did wonder if you were sweet on him — and you are, aren't you?'

'Yes, I am . . . sweet on him.' Ella felt herself flushing again at admitting the fact out loud after keeping it a secret for so long.

'Well, I think that's grand! Now, stop looking as though it's the end of the world, Ella.' Deirdre rubbed Ella's shoulder comfortingly. 'You should tell him, you know. That's what I did. The moment I realised what I felt for Pat, I marched up to him and told him. In fact, if you take my advice, you'll tell Nat today. If you're not careful, that brother of yours will whisk you back to England before you know where you are, and then where will you be? On the other side of the world, that's what!'

'Oh, no, Deirdre, I couldn't possibly be so bold . . . '

'Pfft, you English, always hiding your emotions! I've a good mind to tell him about it myself.'

'Deirdre, don't you dare!'

The two girls continued in this vein as they trudged slowly back to their camp, carrying the heavy bucket between them. They dropped the bucket when they reached the camp.

'Pat, we're back!' Deirdre called out as she walked towards her tent. 'Pat?' There was no answer. 'Pat?' she repeated, her voice louder. There was a trace of worry in her tone. 'Is your back hurting?' She entered the tent she shared with Pat. Ella stayed outside.

'Ella, come here!' Deirdre suddenly

cried out. Ella hurried to the tent and lifted the flap.

The sight that met her eyes froze her with horror. Pat lay still on the ground. His eyes were closed and there was blood on his forehead and on the side of his face.

Beside him, the dirt floor had been dug up, and their gold — the gold they had all worked so hard to bring up from the depths of the earth — was gone.

10

With the assistance of Christopher and Nathaniel, who arrived at the camp shortly afterwards, Pat was gently laid on his bunk. Mrs Gibson and Mrs Barrett, hearing the outcry, offered to fetch fresh water, thus leaving Ella free to race for the doctor's tent. Thankfully he was in, and after examining Pat, the doctor pronounced that he was suffering concussion but that he should recover with rest.

Ella, Christopher, and Nathaniel left the Milligans' tent, leaving Deirdre alone with Pat and the doctor. Mrs Gibson had already sent one of her young sons to fetch the police. After being reassured that there was nothing else they could do, Mrs Gibson and Mrs Barrett returned to their camps.

Christopher was furious. 'Poor Pat

— and what about our gold? Will we get it back?'

'I can't say, Matthews,' Nathaniel said, his voice weary. 'There's not much we can do until we've spoken to the police.'

While the doctor had been examining Pat, Nathaniel had questioned Mrs Barrett and the Gibsons. All of them said they'd noticed two loiterers around — Mrs Barrett had actually brandished a frying pan at them and they had hastily left — but no one had got close enough to gain a clear description of them. Both had worn big hats pulled low over their faces, and they were dressed as diggers.

'I'm glad Pat isn't worse injured! That's the main thing!' Ella declared, after Nathaniel had given them this information.

'Yes, I'm glad too, Ella, of course I am.' Christopher scuffed the dirt angrily with the toe of his boot. 'It's just the thought that after all our hard work, after all that we've achieved, that some scum dares to come along and help himself to our gold — it makes my blood boil!'

Ella had never seen her brother so fierce.

Deirdre came out to join them. 'It's Dr Turner's opinion that Pat was taken by surprise. He had his back to whoever had come into the tent and . . . ' She blanched as another thought occurred to her. 'If Pat was facing them, he'd have put up a fight. I know he would have. The outcome could have been so different.'

Ella placed a comforting arm around Deirdre's shoulders. Yes, it could have been worse. As it was, the robbers had worked quickly. They had struck Pat, taken the gold, and left. It had probably all been accomplished in minutes.

'Is this the Milligan party?' A police sergeant, accompanied by a young constable, was approaching them. They were on foot, leading their horses carefully in between the camp sites.

'We are,' Deirdre answered.

'Sergeant Angell,' the sergeant introduced himself. 'Mrs Milligan, I presume.' Deirdre nodded. 'A young lad has informed me that you've been robbed, and your husband injured.'

Deirdre confirmed that, and told Sergeant Angell what had happened.

At the end of the tale, the sergeant scratched his chin. 'There's also been another robbery today, not too far from here. That digger too was knocked clean out. Whoever these robbers are, they've become confident enough to carry out their attacks in broad daylight. There was even that attempt at the gold escort two months ago, although that's one of their failures, heavily guarded as it is. What worries me is that they're becoming ruthless — anyone who puts up a fight is struck down. They don't seem to care what injuries they inflict. Your man is very, very lucky, Mrs Milligan.'

'Will we get our gold back?' Christopher wanted to know.

'That I don't know, sir,' Sergeant

Angell said. 'I have a few leads I'm working on. I suspect that this particular pair are posing as diggers.'

'Posing as diggers! is that all you have?' Christopher made an angry noise and turned away.

'Christopher, please!' Ella said, but her brother ignored her, striding to his tent. He flung open the tent flap and went in.

Ella understood how he felt. She was angry herself. The robbers had injured Pat and had stolen the fruits of their hard labour. It was enough to make anyone furious.

'Do you have a description, anything?' Nathaniel asked the sergeant. 'I asked, but all I managed to get was that there were two men seen lurking about. No one seems able to give a clear description.'

'Now there I have the advantage.' With a flourish, Sergeant Angell extracted a notebook from his pocket. 'I have a description of one of the robbers. Got it after the Hodges' party were robbed last week . . . now, where did I write it down? Yes, here it is. One of the men was described as dark haired, stocky, with a scar. Just along here.' He gestured along his cheek. 'Like that, sort of jagged. But strangely enough, there's no description of the other man. It's as if he's invisible, but of course that's impossible . . . '

Ella didn't hear the rest of Sergeant Angell's sentence as it registered that the man he had described was a perfect description of Maskell.

'I've seen that man, Sergeant, the one you've just described, the one with the scar. His name is Maskell,' Ella said.

The sergeant turned and looked at her. 'Maskell? Indeed. And where did you see this Maskell, Miss . . . ?'

'Matthews,' Ella said, and ploughed on. 'I've seen him at John Marwood's store tent. He's the coffee and tea merchant.'

'John Marwood. Yes, I know who you mean.' Sergeant Angell regarded Ella with interest and not a little respect. 'That is interesting, Miss Matthews. Very interesting indeed.'

* * *

Pat announced the following morning that he was feeling better, although he did confess he still had a dreadful headache and felt quite dizzy when he tried to stand up.

'No, you most certainly are not getting up today! Nor tomorrow, either!' Deirdre told him sternly, and no matter how much Pat protested, she forced him to stay abed. 'You'll help none of us by making yourself more ill than you are already.'

Deirdre was worried but putting on a brave face, Ella saw.

'I'm fine, Ella,' Deirdre said later when Ella enquired how she was. 'We've been through hard times before. We'll get through this one, too.'

'Of course you will!' Ella said. 'And there's still gold in the mine.'

'The mine that, as of next week, will no longer be ours,' Deirdre reminded her. 'Pat's sold it, so we'll have to start all over again from scratch.' She dashed away angry tears. 'That means digging, and crawling about in darkness, and danger, and cradling, and eating mutton and chasing away flies and living in the dirt and not being able to wash properly . . . ' Making an angry sound, she turned away.

Christopher and Nathaniel returned to the camp at midday.

'There's still gold down there,' Nathaniel said. 'Unfortunately we won't be able to collect much in the time we have left — we just don't have the time to dig further down.'

'And that means we'll have to start all over again!' Christopher kicked angrily at a stone. 'What I'd like to do to those creatures! We worked so hard, and to have it snatched from us like that is — '

'Sergeant Angell will do everything he can to find them,' Ella began.

Christopher snorted. 'Policemen! They're probably no better than the plods in London.'

Ella thought her brother was wrong.

Sergeant Angell seemed far from a fool to her, and he seemed very interested in the information she had given him. She wondered if Sergeant Angell knew more than he had revealed to them, but he did say that he suspected the robbers were posing as diggers.

Did he truly think that? Ella remembered how interested he seemed in John Marwood.

Ella remembered something else. On the night of the dance, Nathaniel himself had told her that Marwood was under the observation of the police. Yet Marwood was a merchant, not a digger . . . but he did know Maskell.

Ella couldn't imagine the pernickety John Marwood lurking about the goldfields, intent on violence and robbery. He just didn't seem the type — although Maskell certainly was!

It wouldn't surprise Ella in the least to discover that John Marwood, even if he did not physically participate in the robberies himself, did have some connection with the gold thieves.

* ★ ★

The next few days passed in a blur for Ella. Conscious of the limited time they had left, the Milligan party — although without the Milligans themselves — worked feverishly at the mine. Pat's recovery was a slow one, and Deirdre spent most of her time attending him.

Christopher channelled his anger into work. He and Nathaniel were taking it in turns to go down into the shaft.

Ella feared her brother was taking unnecessary risks. Ever since the robbery, he seemed to be always simmering with anger.

'Gold is not working risking your life for!' she implored as Christopher began to lower himself rather recklessly into the shaft by the rope ladder. 'Please be careful. I'd rather have a penniless brother than a dead one!'

Something in Ella's voice must have penetrated Christopher's cloud of anger. His grip on the ladder became softer. He looked up at her. 'Of course you're right. I'll be careful, Ella. I promise.'

'Make sure you are,' Ella said sternly, watching as her brother went more carefully down the rope steps. He gave it a shake upon reaching the bottom, and Ella breathed an audible sigh of relief.

'I'll go down later and make sure he's behaving himself,' Nathaniel said.

Ella turned to him thankfully. 'Will you? I'm surprised at Christopher. He's always had fits and starts, but he's never behaved in this fashion.'

'He's suffered a disappointment. He's expended all his hopes on this gamble, won, and then lost. Now he has to start all over again. It's understandable.'

Ella thought about this. 'I understand too, in a way,' She stared down into the darkness as she began to turn the windlass, sending the empty bucket down into the depths of the mine. 'But gold isn't everything. I'd rather have

Christopher safe and sound than racketing about down there, and possibly injuring himself.'

'I'll have a word with him, remind him he has a sister to look after.'

Ella glanced at Nathaniel. His expression was grim.

She returned her gaze to the mine shaft. By his words Nathaniel had just confirmed that he thought of her as Christopher's responsibility!

Silence was maintained until Christopher tugged the rope, indicating the bucket was full. Nathaniel took over the windlass, while Ella brought forward the wheelbarrow.

Outwardly calm but inwardly distressed, Ella continued with her work. Nathaniel helped her down to the creek before returning to the mine. She stared after Nathaniel's retreating figure as she began to rock the cradle.

It wasn't only Christopher who had changed since the robbery; Nathaniel had too. He had become distant. Ella expected him to announce at any moment his intention of returning to Sydney.

And Pat seemed to have had the stuffing knocked out of him. Dear, kind, calm Pat, so seldom ruffled by anything and who Ella doubted had ever hurt a fly. He now spent the days lying on his bunk, his face turned to the wall. Deirdre was frantic with worry.

As for Ella herself, she seemed always to be on the brink of tears. She wanted nothing so much as to sink to her knees and howl.

It wasn't only the gold the thieves had taken, Ella reflected. They had also stolen the spirit of the Milligan party.

Nathaniel's return to the creek broke Ella's musing.

'How much gold do we have?' he enquired.

Ella indicated the bucket where she had put the gold. It was less than the amount they had collected the previous week. Exhausted, she sat down on an upturned bucket, taking out the water flask from her pocket. She poured some into a tin cup and handed it to Nathaniel.

'That's it, then,' Nathaniel said despondently. 'You'll have enough gold to keep you for the next month or so if you're frugal.'

'Yes,' Ella sighed. 'Thank you for staying with us,' she went on quietly. 'I don't think we could have managed without your help, with Pat the way he is.'

'I wouldn't think of leaving you at a time like this!'

'Mr Lake . . . ' Ella ventured. 'Surely you'll be returning to Sydney?'

Nathaniel stared at his cup. 'I'll have to, sooner or later. It's my home, and where my career is.'

'Your editor must be quite cross at your prolonged absence.'

'Perhaps he is.' Suddenly Nathaniel smiled. It lightened his tired features. 'I've been gone so long he's probably busily interviewing new journalists to take my place even as we speak!'

'You shouldn't joke about it,' Ella

said crossly. 'You're the only one of us who will have a steady income, something to go back to. You mustn't jeopardise it.'

He raised his brows. 'Why, Ella, do you want me to leave?' His voice took on a strange tone. Did he sound disappointed? Surely not!

'Yes . . . no . . . oh, it's none of my business, of course.' Ella looked down in confusion. 'You will do as you please.'

'I will indeed, and it pleases me to stay here in Ballarat a while longer . . . and although I'm not doing any writing, I do in fact have a fund of stories that I'll eventually write. You may not realise it, Ella, but you've become a part of Australia's history. We're no longer just a penal settlement. The gold discoveries have forced the world to take notice of us, and people with a convict past will be accepted as citizens of this country. People like my parents who, though they were convicts, are building this nation . . . '

Nathaniel stopped.

Ella remained silent. She had wondered if Nathaniel's parents had been convicts and she now had her answer. And it didn't change the way she felt for him in the slightest.

Nathaniel drank the last of his water and stood up. 'And as for our future, Ella, I think we'd best return to work!'

★ ★ ★

That night, their sleep was abruptly shattered by a woman's loud scream.

Ella bolted upright in bed. There was the sound of men arguing, then a gunshot. Heart hammering, Ella reached down to the floor beside her, lighting the lamp that was always kept by her bedside.

The blanket that partitioned the tent was lifted. Nathaniel looked down at Ella. 'I'll see what's happened. Stay here.'

The woman was now wailing. Loud voices were demanding to know what was going on. Nathaniel abruptly left the tent. Recalling all the violence that had recently occurred, Ella reached for her shawl, intending to follow him.

'No! Stay here, Ella.' Christopher ordered.

'I want to know what's happening.' The woman's wails were louder now.

'Nat will tell us soon enough.' Christopher shivered. 'I don't think it's good.' Side by side, brother and sister sat on the bed in silence.

The tent flap lifted. Ella looked up expectantly, but it was Deirdre.

'Something's happened to the Barretts,' she told them. 'A big crowd has gathered around their tent.'

'Do you know anything?' Ella asked.

Deirdre shook her head. 'No. But I saw Mrs Gibson go inside.'

Despite the gloom, Ella could see how white Deirdre's face was.

'What are the police doing? Why haven't they arrested these robbers?' Deirdre said in a rush.

Ella went over and coaxed her to sit

down on a crate. 'I'm sure they're working on it. These robbers obviously know what they're doing and . . . '

Suddenly the tent flap lifted and Nathaniel entered the tent. He too looked pale.

'That was the Barretts,' he told them. 'They've been robbed. Unfortunately, that's not all.' He sat down on a crate. 'As the robber left, Barrett went after him. He was shot.'

Ella gasped.

'I'm afraid he's dead,' Nathaniel said gently.

Deirdre cried out. Ella sat back down on her bed, suddenly feeling her legs unable to support her. She hadn't known Mr Barrett well, as he spent most of his time down his mine, but he had seemed a nice man. Mrs Barrett, whom she had known better and liked, would be devastated.

'Poor Mrs Barrett,' she said. 'I should go to her.'

'She has Mrs Gibson with her, and another woman. The doctor gave her something to make her sleep.'

'You said 'robber',' Christopher broke in. 'There was only one man?'

'So I understand, from the little Mrs Barrett was able to tell us.' Nathaniel frowned. 'Is it one of the pair who have been carrying out these recent robberies, or a different one? I don't know. She wasn't able to give a description. I understand that their bags were taken, Barrett woke up and in the struggle was shot.'

Deirdre stood up. 'I must return to Pat. He'll be fretting.' She turned and left the tent.

'One of the Gibson boys has gone to fetch the police. They should be here shortly. We'd best go back to bed and try and get some sleep. There's nothing we can do,' Nathaniel said heavily.

Exhausted as she was, Ella found it difficult to find sleep. She couldn't stop thinking of Mr Barrett — or of poor Mrs Barrett, who was now a widow.

★　★　★

Two days later, the last of the tea was drunk, and they had been out of coffee for days. As Deirdre was still nursing Pat, it was up to Ella to make the dreaded journey to Marwood's store, a journey she had hoped never to take again.

Marwood wasn't at the counter when she arrived, but there were voices coming from inside the tent. One of them was distinctly Marwood's — and he sounded furious.

Hardly daring to breathe and leaning as far over the counter as she dared, Ella peeked between the tent flaps and glimpsed Marwood and Maskell, heads bent close together. They were talking too quietly for Ella to make out what they were saying, but it was clear that Marwood was extremely displeased with his companion.

Suddenly Maskell lifted his hand. He shook it in Marwood's face.

What he held made Ella gasp. The sound she made must have been audible, because the pair of them turned around.

Quickly taking a step back from the counter, Ella affected a casualness she did not feel.

'Good morning, Mr Marwood,' she said as Marwood lifted the tent flap and came to the counter. Ella hoped he would think she had just arrived at his tent. Her palms began to sweat and her heart thudded in nervousness. Did he suspect her of overhearing his conversation with Maskell?

If Marwood was disconcerted to see Ella at his store tent, he gave no outward show of it. Pasting his customary fulsome smile to his face, he nodded a greeting at her and waved a dismissal at Maskell. The stocky man, pulling his jacket up around his ears and tugging his slouch hat low over his face, stomped grumpily from the tent. He looked to be in a bad temper. Ella sensed that if she had been in his way this time, he would have knocked her flat to the ground.

'Good morning, Miss Matthews. How can I help you?' Marwood's smile didn't falter. He didn't appear angry now; on the contrary, he seemed his usual amiable self — although Ella thought she detected a flush in his skin.

Ella gave her order. She was pleased to note that she spoke in her usual tone, managing to hide the nervousness she still felt. Marwood disappeared into his tent, and quickly reappeared with the requested packets of tea and coffee. Not immediately handing them to Ella, he began chattering in his usual fashion.

Ella affected to listen to him, nodding and saying 'yes' and 'no' at appropriate moments, but all the time he was talking to her, she covertly studied him. She had already noted how well dressed John Marwood always was, but truly he was far better dressed than any of the other merchants on the goldfields, some of whom were positively slovenly.

He seemed to eat well too. Ella had seen foods of all description at his store, food she had rarely seen during her time on the goldfields, let alone eaten. If one wanted to eat well, one had to pay handsomely. So how did he manage to pay for his comforts?

It had to be from the profits of selling illegal alcohol. John Marwood seemed too ordinary, too nondescript, to indulge in other forms of skulduggery. It took a feat of imagination to connect him with an act of violence. He just didn't seem the sort; he was the type of man one would not take a second look at. Yet Ella had always suspected — as did Deirdre — that beneath his veneer of joviality there lurked a vastly different character.

'Yes, you do indeed seem to be doing very well,' she agreed as Marwood again made his customary remarks about his success on the goldfields. Finally he handed her the tea and coffee.

Ella paid him and tucked the packets of coffee and tea into her basket. She was now eager to leave his company, yet it wouldn't do to turn and flee. She forced herself to be patient. Marwood always had more to say.

He preened; he couldn't seem to help himself. 'As I think I've mentioned to you many times before, Miss Matthews, canny merchants do well!'

Another minute passed before Ella was able to make her farewells and depart. She walked at a steady pace, although she longed to lift her skirts and run. She fancied she felt Marwood's eyes boring into her back.

Once out of sight of Marwood's tent, Ella ran. She had important information.

What she had seen Maskell holding was one of Pat's leather pouches, the initials 'P. M.' clearly embroidered on it — the pouches where Pat had kept their gold.

11

The moment Ella returned to the camp, she told Nathaniel what she had seen. Nathaniel was uneasy. 'Are you certain Marwood didn't see you looking at Maskell holding that pouch? Think, Ella!'

Ella recounted the scene in her mind. From the moment when she had seen the pouch in Maskell's hand, all her attention had been focused upon him. Had Marwood seen her looking at Maskell? As she hadn't looked in his direction, she couldn't say.

'Truly I don't know,' Ella said slowly. 'Maybe not. He was further back in the tent, so perhaps he did not see me. But I cannot say with certainty.'

'Sergeant Angell will have to know about this, and as quickly as possible before Marwood can destroy those pouches. They are evidence of his involvement in the robberies.' Suddenly taking Ella's face between his hands, Nathaniel scrutinised her face. 'Think again, Ella. Did Marwood see you?' He sounded genuinely worried, the concern in his grey eyes evident.

Ella shook her head. 'I can't be sure. But surely he wouldn't waste valuable time coming after me, even if he did suspect me seeing or overhearing something. Marwood isn't stupid. He would destroy those pouches and flee. That's what I would do if I were him!'

Nathaniel released her and stepped back. 'There's no telling what a man of Marwood's stamp would do. He's a braggart and overconfident, but I'd rather he flee the goldfields, even if he does escape justice — for make no mistake, Ella: Marwood is a dangerous man. I don't like leaving you . . . '

He looked around. 'Where is your brother?'

'He's meeting a man who's thinking of selling his mine.'

'Oh, yes. He did say that at breakfast,

I'd forgotten.' Nathaniel lifted his hand and pushed his dark hair off his forehead. 'I'd better go. The sooner Sergeant Angell has this information, the sooner he can act on it — before Marwood has a chance to dispose of the pouches and make his escape!'

He reached forward and clasped Ella's hands briefly. 'I'll return as quickly as I can, Ella. Don't leave the camp.' Then he did a surprising thing. Taking her face between his hands again, he kissed her lips quickly.

And before Ella had a chance to react, Nathaniel was gone.

★   ★   ★

Ella returned to her tent. She sat down on her bed, her thoughts in a whirl. Nathaniel had kissed her!

She forced herself to think sensibly. He meant it as a gesture of comfort and concern for her welfare, that's all. He didn't want her worrying about Marwood. How she wished it were otherwise.

'Ah, Miss Matthews, I was hoping to catch you alone.'

John Marwood's voice cut sharply into Ella's daydream. He was here, in her tent! Absorbed in her thoughts, she hadn't heard him approach.

Though her legs felt distinctly wobbly, Ella rose. Her heart began to thud painfully when she saw he was holding a pistol.

'Sit down, Miss Matthews.' Marwood gestured with the pistol. 'Don't think of screaming or trying to escape. I won't hesitate to shoot if need be.'

'I'm sure you wouldn't.' Ella forced herself to remain calm, although her heart continued to hammer wildly. She sat back down on her bed and clasped her hands in her lap, wondering if Deirdre and Pat were aware of Marwood's presence. She hoped fervently that they weren't; Pat was still ill and incapable of defending himself, let alone both herself and Deirdre.

And it was herself that Marwood was interested in. Ella silently willed

Nathaniel and Sergeant Angell to hurry.

'I saw you looking at Maskell.' Marwood pulled up a crate and seated himself directly in front of Ella. She noticed his hand holding the gun was perfectly steady; he didn't seem agitated in the least. He clearly had nerves of steel! 'Who have you told? Your brother? Your newspaper friend?'

'I don't know what you're talking about, Mr Marwood. Why would I have been looking at Maskell? I don't find him at all pleasant to gaze upon.' Ella was pleased at how calm she sounded.

'This is not a game, Miss Matthews! Answer my question. I want to know if I should make a swift departure. I've made last-minute escapes before, and I can do so again. The trick is to know when to leave, to keep one step ahead of the law.'

'I'm sure you know many tricks. Will you be taking Maskell with you?'

'Maskell can take care of himself. I care not. He was useful once but he's now a liability. He's a fool. I told him to

173

kill only when necessary, and never when the police are sniffing around! How dare he thieve without telling me . . . ' Marwood broke off, looking angry. Ella wasn't sure if it was against herself or Maskell. Probably both, Maskell for not obeying orders and herself for seeing Pat's pouch. The death of Mr Barrett was obviously unimportant to Marwood.

'I thought Maskell was a friend of yours,' Ella said, her voice still calm despite the rage inside her against what had been done to Mr Barrett — and who knew how many others?

'An acquaintance only, Miss Matthews. And so I shall tell the police.'

'I've seen him at your tent before today.'

Marwood raised his almost invisible eyebrows. 'You've been seen at my tent before today as well, Miss Matthews.'

As Marwood didn't seem intent on harming her — or at least not at this moment — Ella decided to continue talking. He was still confident and didn't seem in any hurry to leave. She already knew he liked talking about himself and was a vain man, always boasting of his cleverness.

Ella would fan that vanity. 'I know you've been playing your tricks on other goldfields. How else would you know Mr Lake is a journalist? I've certainly never mentioned him to you, and Deirdre never would. Funnily enough, Mr Lake seems to know you!'

'He does. I recognised Lake the moment I saw him at your little celebration. I confess it gave me a nasty turn to realise he was a member of your party, Miss Matthews. I've seen him on other goldfields, always asking questions, poking and prying into things that are none of his concern, scribbling away in that notebook of his.

'Still, he couldn't help knowing me! I've made quite a name for myself, if that's the right term to use, because nobody knows my real name. I've not used my real name since I served out my sentence and was granted my ticket of leave.'

Ella schooled her expression into one of curiosity, and Marwood laughed harshly. 'Yes, I was once a convict, Miss Matthews, and no, I'm not John Marwood. The real John Marwood was a digger who — well, he met an unfortunate end. But his name has come in useful in Ballarat. I change my name when necessary. I possess the unique ability to blend in with whatever surroundings I find myself in. Names aren't important.'

'You ought to be ashamed yourself!' Ella regarded Marwood with open dislike. 'You live off the proceeds of hard-working folk, and . . . and worse!'

Marwood again raised his pale eyebrows, this time to express astonishment. 'Why should I be ashamed? Really, Miss Matthews, you surprise me! I never suspected you of being obtuse. Ever since I regained my freedom, I've developed an extreme aversion to any type of strenuous activity, but especially an aversion to digging and dirt. And as I've told you on more than one occasion, Ballarat has been kind to me, very kind to me.

'I've enjoyed it here, and I would have been happy to stay longer. Not only because of all the gold I've . . . ah, shall I say, *amassed*, but the selling of grog has turned a very tidy profit.' He preened. 'Yes, I'll be sorry to leave, but needs must — and there are many other ways of parting fools from their money. Now, if you would kindly answer my question, Miss Matthews . . . ' Marwood trailed to a stop as voices and feet were heard outside.

Christopher had returned, and was speaking with Deirdre. Gravel crunched underfoot. Marwood's gaze turned towards the tent flap.

His momentary distraction was all the opportunity Ella needed. Grabbing the heavy rag-stuffed pillow from her bed, she flung it at Marwood's head with all her might. He fell backwards off the crate, the pistol firing harmlessly into the canvas roof of the tent.

As the pistol was flung from his hand, Ella kicked it under her bed, at the same time screaming at the top of her lungs.

Marwood recovered himself quickly. Ignoring his pistol, he scrambled to his feet. Knocking Ella to the ground, he dashed towards the tent flap . . . to run straight into the welcoming arms of Sergeant Angell.

★ ★ ★

The force of the fall knocked Ella's breath from her body. Lying on her side, gasping for breath, the next few moments passed in a whirl of confusion. The tent seemed full of noisy men. Marwood's voice was the loudest, yelling and cursing as he attempted to evade capture. Things were knocked over and trampling feet stirred up the dust.

Fearing that she would be trampled

or kicked by someone's scuffling feet — or choke to death on the dust — Ella attempted to roll out of the way.

'Ella!' Suddenly Nathaniel was there. Dropping to his knees, he gently helped her to sit up. His eyes were full of concern. 'Are you all right?'

Ella nodded shakily. 'Yes.' She reached out a hand and Nathaniel helped her to her feet. She looked around. The tent had emptied as quickly as it had filled. The scuffle had moved outside, and it was evident that it had attracted a curious crowd, judging by the increased noise.

'That was Sergeant Angell I saw, wasn't it?' Ella asked.

'Yes. He wasn't far away, thank heavens, and when I imparted to him what you had seen, he insisted on returning with me instantly, bringing with him four brawny policemen. Like me, he was worried that Marwood might come to confront you, and we were right! But come outside. You'll feel better in the fresh air.'

Fortunately the curious onlookers preferred to follow Sergeant Angell and his policemen as they bore away the still struggling and protesting Marwood, rather than hang about the Milligan camp. Ella sat down on a crate, her legs seeming hardly able to bear her weight. Never in her life had she been threatened with a pistol.

Delayed reaction set in, and Ella burst into tears.

As sobs racked her body, Nathaniel put his arms around her, holding her close, letting her have her cry. After a while, Ella's sobs subsided and Nathaniel released her. Ella felt bereft and lost as he moved away.

'Ella!' Christopher ran towards them. Ella saw that although he had a bloodied nose, he looked distinctly pleased with himself. She wondered if he had given Marwood a bloody nose on his own account!

'You'll be pleased to know that Sergeant Angell has taken Marwood into custody. Maskell was apprehended earlier this morning. The goldfields will be a lot safer now that those two have been arrested — ' He stopped, suddenly noticing his sister's tear-streaked face. 'Ella, are you all right? Did Marwood hurt you? If he has, I'll go after him and hit him again!'

'No, I'm fine, Christopher. It's just the shock, I think.' She quickly told her brother what had occurred in the tent, assuring him that she was unhurt.

Christopher regarded her with concern. 'The sooner we return to England, the better,' he said. 'I've been very irresponsible, Ella. I should never have persuaded you to come out here. You were safe with Mrs Pugh. But things will be different now we have money. We'll buy a house in London, and you can even have a Season, if you wish.' He looked around the goldfields and shuddered. 'Yes, we'll go home as soon as we may.'

★   ★   ★

That night saw another celebration on the goldfields, this time to mark the arrest of John Marwood and Maskell. Mrs Barrett's gold was returned to her, as well as gold belonging to a few other diggers. Marwood had amassed, besides gold, quite an amount of stolen property and it would be a while before it was all sorted out.

Although Ella was equally pleased that the goldfields were now free of those two rogues, she was in a far from celebratory mood.

The happiest people were Pat — now almost fully recovered — and Deirdre. Being reunited with their share of the gold had raised Pat's spirits immensely, and the Milligans' plans for the purchase of a farm could go ahead. Soon they would start the next phase of their new life.

Watching Pat and Deirdre sitting close together, murmuring and laughing, Ella was certain that whatever hardships they faced in the future — and there would be many, given the harsh environment they had chosen to live in — they would face them bravely together, because of the security of their love.

Ella gave a sad sigh. When Nathaniel entered her life, everything turned topsy-turvy. No matter how often she told herself the sooner she returned to England the better, it wasn't becoming any easier to accept.

'You don't look very happy, Ella.' Christopher came and sat beside her.

Ella looked at her brother. He looked content. The thought of going home sat well with him.

Ella wished with all her heart that she could feel the same, but she couldn't. One couldn't summon the impossible.

'You don't want to return home, do you?' Christopher unexpectedly said. 'No, don't deny it,' he went on when Ella opened her mouth to speak. 'I'm your brother, and although I'm not a very observant fellow, I believe I know why. It's Nat, isn't it?'

Ella nodded miserably. 'Yes. So it's

best I go home with you. I'll be all right once I'm home, truly. I know I have no future here, and now we're financially independent we can make a comfortable life for ourselves.'

Christopher took Ella's hand and gave it a squeeze. 'We'll talk tomorrow. You're tired after everything that's happened today. Go and lie down,' he said kindly. 'I'll tell the others you have a headache.'

'Yes, I think I will.' Ella rose to her feet and headed for the tent, silently chiding herself yet again for her foolishness for having fallen in love with Nathaniel — although she was at a loss to explain how she could have stopped herself from doing so!

Yet she was no green girl. She should have been more aware of the direction her feelings were taking so she could have dealt with them sooner. She and Nathaniel were from different worlds. He was as much a part of this harsh country as the gum trees and deserts. She herself was the daughter of gentlefolk, from a rainy country of soft green hills.

She would return to England, her homeland, and never see Nathaniel again. The sooner she accepted that unpalatable fact, the better; she would simply have to become accustomed to living with this aching sense of loss.

Ella resolved to find something to do that would keep her busy, so busy that she wouldn't have time to remember and think and wonder about Nathaniel. Something that would keep her so occupied that it would fill the great void that would be left in her life — some charitable work, perhaps. With luck it would be fulfilling enough so that she would be able to count her blessings, even if Nathaniel was no longer part of her life.

With a deep, sad sigh, Ella lifted the tent flap. She would lie down on her bed and close her eyes. With luck she would fall into a deep sleep and . . .

'Mr Lake!' Ella started. The tent flap closed behind her. 'I'm sorry, I didn't

185

realise you were here. I thought you were outside,' She took a step back, not wishing to be alone with him. She would be unable to hide her feelings, raw as they were.

Nathaniel sprang to his feet, his hand held out. 'Don't go, Ella.' He had been sitting on his side of the tent. A portable writing desk was set on his knees, papers strewn across it. On another crate, a lamp was set.

'I told your brother I didn't intend to attend the celebration,' Nathaniel explained 'I thought I'd use the time more profitably to finish off some articles and please my editor. He must be wondering what I've been doing all these weeks. He probably thinks I've fallen down a mineshaft!'

So Christopher knew Nathaniel was in here working! What did he mean by sending her off to bed?

'Oh,' Ella said, wrong-footed. 'I'll leave you to your work, then.' She turned away, about to lift open the tent flap.

'No, please stay, Ella. I could use your help.'

This was too much! Fearing she was about to cry, Ella swallowed the lump that had somehow lodged in her throat.

Nathaniel looked disappointed when she didn't immediately reply. 'I'm sorry, Ella, I shouldn't have asked such a thing. You must have just come in to fetch something and return to the celebration. Don't worry, I'll manage. I just thought, when you came in, you seemed . . . '

'No, Mr Lake, I don't feel like returning to the celebration. I'm more than happy to stay here and help you.' Ella dragged across the crate from her side of the tent and sat down, setting the portable writing desk on her knees. *Just this one last time*, she thought. Even knowing it was foolish and would only intensify the hurt, this would be the last time she would work with Nathaniel. The memory of it would have to last for the rest of her life.

Nathaniel handed her paper, pen, and ink.

They worked steadily for twenty minutes before Nathaniel spoke again. 'Your brother mentioned that you'll be returning to Melbourne the day after tomorrow, and as soon as he can arrange passage, you'll set sail for England. You must be pleased.'

Ella carefully finished the sentence she was writing before she answered. Christopher hadn't discussed anything with her yet, but she imagined that that was his plan.

'Yes,' she said eventually. There was a world of misery in that one word.

'That 'yes' sounds more like a 'no' to me.'

Ella didn't reply. Dipping the pen in the ink, she began the next sentence. She stared at Nathaniel's scribbled notes. She couldn't make head or tail of them. Suddenly realising that her vision was impaired because her eyes were filled with tears, she angrily blinked them away. The light in the tent was quite dim. With luck, Nathaniel would not have noticed them.

Trying not to sniff, Ella stabbed the pen at the paper and began again.

Her hand veered across the paper, blotching it with ink spots, when Nathaniel abruptly left his crate and came to kneel beside her. He gently took the pen from her suddenly nerveless fingers, and set it down. Taking her chin in his hand, he forced her to look at him.

Ella jerked her head away.

'Ella, look at me,' Nathaniel commanded.

With a great effort of will, Ella did so.

'You don't want to return to England. Can you tell me why?' Nathaniel asked her softly.

'I do want to return to England, Mr Lake. Pray tell me where else should I go, but home?'

'Liar!' Taking Ella's ink-smeared hand, he kissed it. 'As to where you should make your home, why should it not be here in Australia? In Sydney, to be more precise?'

'Sydney?' Ella squeaked. 'What are you talking about, Mr Lake? Sydney is where you live.'

'It is indeed. And I would very much like it to be your home as well, Ella. I want you to meet my parents, my brothers, and my sisters.' Nathaniel took a deep breath. 'I'm asking you to marry me, Ella!'

'Marry you?' Ella's mind whirled. She tried to order her thoughts. 'You want to marry me? Why?'

'Why?' Nathaniel took her shoulders and gave them a gentle shake. 'Because I love you, Ella. I cannot bear the thought of you returning to England. It's all I've been thinking of for weeks. It's why I've stayed with you, not returning to Sydney when I should have done so weeks ago.'

Suddenly, his expression became uncertain. 'Am I mistaken? I told you my parents were convicts. That doesn't mean they are evil people. They weren't even criminals. They stole because they were hungry, and because of that, they were transported to Australia. When they had served their sentence, they could not return to England, so they resolved to make the best life they could for themselves here, and they have. Could you make a new life here with me, Ella?

'I thought I was content, living as I was, travelling here and there at the behest of my paper. Now I feel incomplete. I can hardly bear the thought of never seeing you again, and you've been so unhappy these past weeks, I began to hope that you might feel the same. Am I correct, my dearest Ella? Or have I been imagining things? Do you feel for me what I feel for you?'

A bubble of joy was forming deep inside Ella as she listened to Nathaniel's words, and suddenly she found her voice. 'Oh, Nathaniel, I do. I love you. It matters not to me that your parents were once convicts, I know I will like them and the rest of your family, because I love you. No, you haven't been imagining things. I love you so much, my heart was breaking at the thought of returning to England and never seeing you again. It is my dearest wish to make my home with you. I hardly dare believe it . . . '

'Believe it, Ella. It's true.' Then Nathaniel took her in his arms and kissed her. Ella kissed him back with all the yearning she had been so careful to conceal for so long. Her misery dissolved. Nathaniel loved her, he wanted to marry her and she would be with him for the rest of her life.

After a long while had passed, Nathaniel still held Ella in his arms. They sat quietly together, listening to the celebration still going on outside. Neither of them felt the slightest inclination to go outside and join in.

'Marrying me means you may not see your brother ever again, Ella,' Nathaniel said.

'I know.' Ella moved away a little to look Nathaniel in the face. 'But I've never been more sure of anything in my life.' And she was, although Ella knew she would miss Christopher. She would miss England, too . . . But perhaps she would see Christopher again one day. After all, hadn't Nathaniel told her that he would like to see Europe? Perhaps they would be granted the opportunity to travel there together one day; it wasn't inconceivable . . . and as Ella now knew, miracles did happen!

But England was no longer Ella's home. The thought caused her no regrets. She had a new home now, a new home in a new country, with the man she loved more than life itself.

And Ella was content that it should be so.